Fatal Fantasy

Books by Jane Tesh

The Grace Street Mysteries
Stolen Hearts
Mixed Signals
Now you See It
Just You Wait
Baby, Take a Bow
Death by Dragonfly
Gone Daddy Blues

The Madeline Maclin Mysteries
A Case of Imagination
A Hard Bargain
A Little Learning
A Bad Reputation
Evil Turns
A Wild Ride

Fatal Fantasy

Grace Street Mystery #8

Jane Tesh

Savvy Press

First Edition 2021

Library of Congress Control Number: 2021945687

ISBN: 9781939113542   Trade Paperback
ISBN: 9781939113535   Kindle

Savvy Press
479 Beattie Hollow Rd
Salem NY 12865
www.savvypress.com
info@savvypress.com

www.janetesh.com

Cover design: François Thisdale

Printed in the United States of America

Chapter titles are the names of classic science fiction and fantasy movies, the kind Randall and Camden especially enjoy. Many of the other books, TV shows, and movies mentioned are fictional.

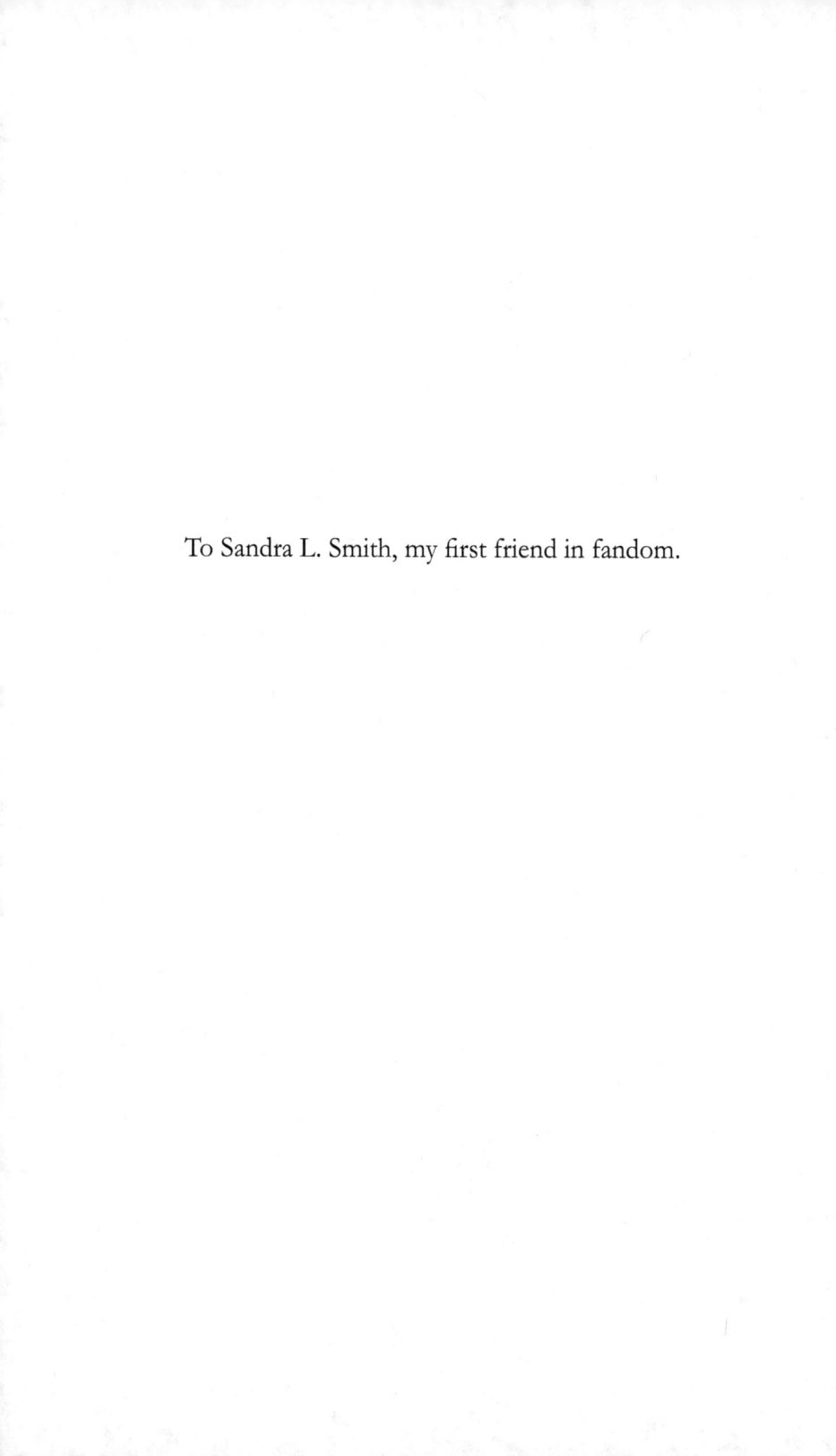

To Sandra L. Smith, my first friend in fandom.

Acknowledgements

Another huge thank you to my excellent team: editor Ellen Larson, proofreader Linda Parks, and cover artist Francois Thisdale.

CHAPTER ONE

"Have Rocket, Will Travel"

Joy and excitement had come at last to 302 Grace Street: Parkland, NC, had been chosen to host the winter Science Fiction and Fantasy ExtravaganzaCon. So that chilly Friday morning in January, Camden and I were sitting in the island (our name for the comfortable area in the middle of our living room), phones in hand, gleefully scrolling through the online program of events, making our final choices. I was in my usual seat, the faded blue armchair, and Camden was in his regular spot on the green corduroy sofa.

Things were not always this cheerful. This past November I had made a lot of noise about giving up and quitting the detective business. I was tired of dealing with deadbeat dads and full of self-doubt about my ability to make any kind of difference. Camden had used falling off the roof and a mild concussion as an excuse to not be psychic—another round of Why Can't I Be Normal? It was Funk Month for both of us. But thanks to the encouraging spirit of my little daughter Lindsey, I was back on track. Besides catching a serial killer, I'd solved quite a few cases in the past weeks, and now I could reward myself with the bizarre extravaganza that was a week-long multi-genre convention, which included all forms of science-fiction, fantasy, gaming, comics, and psychic phenomena.

Camden and I were fans of old science fiction movies. He also liked anime, and we'd been known to play a video game or two, so we were raring to go.

"Okay, so we'll catch the pilot episode of *Doorway to Mars.* Damn, you never see that any more. That's at nine." I put the information into my phone.

Camden scrolled down the page. "*Vampire Rage* at eleven."

"Check."

"Don't forget I want to meet Iris Hudson, too. She's signing her latest *Dark Star* book from three to five."

"Got it." I scrolled down to a full page photo of a curvaceous blonde. "'Get Your Picture Taken With Lucinda Love.' Lucinda, you are first on my list, thanks to that green lizard skin bikini."

"A display of props from *Galaxy Kings.* How'd I miss that?"

"Look!" He turned his phone so I could see. "They've got one of the original Gorbo costumes. That thing used to creep me out as a kid."

Camden's wife Ellin paused on her way from the island to the kitchen. She had on one of her dark blue power suits that made her short curls look like polished gold and gave her blue eyes an added glare. "Speaking of kids, you two are worse than children."

"Ellie, this is a major event," Camden said. "Seven days of multi-genre delight."

"Fine. Just don't forget Mother's tea at three o'clock."

Camden looked up, eyes wide. "Three o'clock tomorrow?"

"Yes, and you promised you'd get a haircut."

He gulped. "Ellie, honey—"

"You promised weeks ago. You said you'd sing all of Mother's favorite songs."

"But the convention—"

"You'll be there all morning, and you can go back after the tea."

She didn't have to say anything else. He was stuck and he knew it. She went into the kitchen. Camden gazed after her with a forlorn expression.

I had to know. "And Mother's favorite songs are?"

"'You Light Up My Life,' 'Wind Beneath My Wings,' stuff like that. 'Scarlet Ribbons.'"

"'Feelings'?"

"No, thank goodness. 'Try to Remember.' 'Danny Boy.'"

"Well, you have fun singing all those mushy songs while I lock lips with Lucinda Love, Lizard Vixen from the Planet Viagra."

"I don't know why I forgot the tea was the first day of the con."

"Because secretly you do not want to go to Mother's tea."

He sighed and ran his hands through the pale mop he calls his hair. He keeps it fairly short in back, but when it starts flopping too far over his eyes, Ellin starts complaining. Most women oo and ahh. You can see their fingers itching to touch it, but Ellin's way too concerned with appearances.

Even I had to admit it was floppier than usual.

Camden's glance told me he'd read that thought. In fact, he can read most of my thoughts, which can be annoying and occasionally helpful.

"Okay, so maybe it needs a trim," he said.

"Only if Jean and her friends want to see your eyes as you emote."

Ellin's mother, Jean, the single-serving size portion of Ellin, had finally come to grips with having a psychic son-in-law. She did this by ignoring his talent, referring to his visions as "fits." I'm sure the only vision Jean ever had in her life was of Ellin walking down the aisle with a doctor, lawyer, or senator, certainly not a psychic who worked part time in a clothing store. But she did admire his voice. She was very happy to show him off at her social soirees and country club dos. This was an easy way for Camden to keep peace in the family, because he loved to sing, as I reminded him. "How long do you have to sing? An hour, maybe? That's not as bad as it could be."

"Jean likes to introduce me to everybody. It could take weeks."

"Say you have another engagement. That'll be the truth."

Camden can't lie worth a damn. He had these large blue eyes that might as well be TelePrompTers, so deception was impossible. "I suppose it would."

"Ellin's giving that chain a little slack, pal. Take advantage of it."

Camden's eyes were now saying back off, buster. But it was true. He was insanely in love with his wife and did almost everything she said. Part of this was to keep her happy, and the residents of 302 Grace were grateful for his intervention, and part of it was because he truly wanted to please her. As a survivor of two divorces, I found this kind of behavior unsettling, but I had to admit Ellin took care of him, and the occasional Deep Kisses she laid on him were works of art.

He sighed again and picked up his program book. "Let's see what I can get in."

"You still have six other days."

"Yes, but Saturday's opening day. You know how that is."

Stuart King, currently our only tenant, came puffing down the stairs. Stuart was short and bald and could have easily been cast as the cheerful yet clueless boss on any sitcom. He was an actor of sorts who dressed up in various oversized animal and inanimate object costumes for parties. The rest of the time, he worked as assistant manager at one of the Super Food stores. This was handy because with the limited cash flow around Grace Street, the dented cans and crushed boxes of cereal he brought home were most welcome.

"Hey, you guys are going to ExtravaganzaCon tomorrow, right?"

"Just finalizing our plans," I said. "We want to be there when it opens at eight. We'll see you and your fellow Klingons there."

Stuart gargled something I assumed was Klingon for "okay."

Ellin returned carrying the large thermos she used to transport vast quantities of caffeine to and from work. "Oh, one other thing, Cam. Sean and Geoff Snyder are in town for the convention. They're coming to the studio today. You promised you'd speak to them."

Camden fell back on the sofa, clutching his chest as if shot. Ellin wasn't impressed by the dramatics.

"Who are they?" Stuart asked.

"Two guys who make a living debunking psychics," I said. "Two guys who can't spell their names right." Sean I always liked to call "Seen," and Geoff, "Gee-off."

"Oh," Stuart said. "They want to see if Cam's a fake."

"Yes," Ellin said, "and they'll be very sorry."

Camden sat up. "Ellie, no matter what I do or say, they'll believe what they want."

"I want to prove to them there really is such a thing as psychic ability."

"Isn't there another psychic hanging around you can use?"

"No, there isn't."

That was because, ironically enough, no one who worked for the Psychic Service Network had any psychic talent.

Even though he knew it was useless, Camden kept trying. "Are you sure you want to film this?"

"Of course. It'll make a great show." She took a drink of coffee, not that she needed re-charging. "You owe me."

I don't know how either of them kept track of who owed what, but apparently, Camden was on the losing side this month.

"I thought since Christmas we were even."

She smiled the smile of one who knew she had the upper hand. "You're still working off that serial killer."

Game, set, and match to Ellin. "What time today?" he said.

"Randall can bring you over at three-thirty."

I indicated her giant thermos. "Didn't the doctor tell you to cut down on the caffeine?"

I'm used to her glares, but this one was particularly frosty. "Is that really any of your business?"

Camden was thrilled and delighted by the idea of being a father. Ellin was not happy about being pregnant. It interfered with her work.

"I'm only five months," she continued, "and the doctor says everything is fine."

"That's because the baby's zonked all the time."

Camden didn't say anything, but the concerned look in his eyes made her reconsider. "I'll see if I can get by with a little less." She took one last sip. "Three-thirty. Don't be late."

Stuart went back upstairs to find his Klingon costume, passing Kary as she came down the stairs, carrying her school tote bag.

As usual, she looked radiant, her long silky blonde hair tied back in a braid, revealing silver earrings shaped like snowflakes. She had on a gray skirt and a blue sweater with a pattern of little white snowflakes. The perfect January outfit for a second grade teacher. Although Kary enjoyed teaching, she had plans to become a guidance counselor, but finding the classes she needed and finding time to attend them was rough going.

"All set for ExtravaganzaCon tomorrow, David?"

"You bet," I said. "Want to go?"

She set the tote bag down and took her coat from the hall tree in the foyer. "Sure. Sounds like fun." My office phone rang, and since she was closest to the door, she said, "I'll get it."

Camden and I heard a brief conversation, and then she came out. Her face was so pale, I was afraid she was going to faint.

I jumped up. "What is it? What's wrong?"

"It's my father. He's in trouble. He wants to talk to you."

I didn't want to talk to him. This was the man who had cut Kary completely off from her family, a preacher so rigidly fundamentalist that when his own daughter was almost dying from complications of an unplanned pregnancy he couldn't bring himself to help or forgive her.

"Do you want me to help him?"

I'd never seen her look so miserable. "Yes. I don't want to be like him. I don't want to be the one who turns him away."

I went into my office and picked up the phone. "Mr. Ingram, this is David Randall. How may I help you?"

The man's voice was terse. "It's *Pastor* Ingram, and I don't wish to discuss anything over the phone. Can we talk in your office?"

My office was in a downstairs parlor in our home, and I sure as hell didn't want this man at 302 Grace. "Do you know Perkie's Coffee Shop in the Willow Street Park? I can meet you there."

"Very well. I'll expect you there in ten minutes."

Of course, your majesty. "All right."

He hung up and so did I. Kary stood in the doorway. "Do you know what this is about, Kary?"

"He didn't tell me. I guess he thought I was your secretary."

He didn't even recognize his daughter's voice. "Does he know you live here?"

"He doesn't know anything about me."

"But you want me to help him."

She took a long time to answer and finally said, "Yes."

***

Kary must have gotten her looks from her mother. Gary Neil Ingram—excuse me—Pastor Gary Neil Ingram was an overweight man in his fifties with sparse pale hair. His features crowded together in the middle of a fleshy red face, small narrow eyes, a sharp nose, and a pinched-looking mouth. His manner suggested he was used to getting his way and didn't care who he had to bulldoze to get it.

"I expect complete discretion on your part, Mr. Randall."

"I wouldn't be in this business if I couldn't keep a secret. How did you hear about my agency?"

"One of my wife's friends suggested you. I assure you my problem is far more serious."

We sat down at one of the small tables in the coffee shop. Pastor Ingram folded his large arms. He reminded me of a troll guarding a bridge, and by damn, no one was going to cross. "Someone is out to ruin me and destroy all of God's work I have done in this city."

"How are they doing that?"

"Outrageous pictures of an imposter have surfaced on the Internet. Someone claiming to be the Angel of Truth parodies my sermons and my television programs on YouTube, putting evil words in my mouth and defiling all that is good and righteous!"

I'd seen the *Ingram Bible Hour*. The program was hard to miss when channel surfing because it was on all day. I'd caught little snippets of Pastor Gary screaming and waving his Bible. "Do you have any idea who would want to do this?"

"Don't you think if I knew, I would have choked the Devil out of them by now?"

None of this forgive-thy-neighbor stuff for Pastor Gary. "I'll need a list of people you've argued with recently. Have you received any threats?"

"I am constantly bombarded by unbelievers. Why do you think I work so diligently to bring God's message to the world? I'm sure there are thousands of people who would like to have me silenced."

"If I'm going to be useful, you're going to have to cut that down to a manageable number."

He sighed an exasperated sigh. "I suppose I can't expect you to interview thousands."

"Thanks."

His eyes narrowed even further. "Are you a Christian, Mr. Randall?"

"I go to church." So I can sit beside your daughter.

"That doesn't answer my question."

Good luck finding a Christian detective. "How about this? I solve your case, and you can convert me."

He didn't like my flippant attitude, but he also wanted my help. "Start with Eric O'Conner, one of my outreach program assistants. He overstepped the boundaries and I had to fire him recently. There was something fishy about him from the start, something weird."

"Weird in what way?"

"Overly personal. Always asking impertinent questions. I wouldn't put it past him to try to blackmail me."

"Are you being blackmailed?"

"Not yet."

I wrote down the name. "What about your TV channel? Do you get any hate mail?"

"Occasionally. We do not avoid controversy. There is only one way to salvation, Mr. Randall, and I am determined to make people see it."

Oh, people love being told what to do. It was clear he was oblivious to the effect he had on people. "I'd like to come by your church office and talk to your employees. Freedom Path, correct?"

He frowned and corrected me. "Freedom Path United Church of the Revelation, yes. We are always open." He got up. "Call me as soon as you have results."

"Hold on," I said. "There's a little matter of my fee."

He looked affronted. "This is for the church. This is for God's work."

"No, this is for you. It's your problem, your image that's on the Internet. If you can't afford to hire me, then find someone else." Someone who'd feel sorry for you, which I didn't.

He wavered. I knew that like all televangelists, he was wealthy and most of his wealth came from contributions from his flock. "Very well. But I expect a swift solution."

"I'll do my best. I'll need contact information on O'Conner."

"My secretary will have that for you when you stop by the church." He sat back down and grudgingly wrote a check. I controlled an almost overwhelming urge to punch him in his fat gut. Pastor Gary had been living like a king while Kary struggled and scraped along on her teacher's salary. I definitely wanted to find this Angel of Truth, mainly to shake the angel's hand. But I had a job to do and enough professional pride to give it my best shot.

CHAPTER TWO

"Assignment Outerspace"

When I got home, Camden was waiting at the front door.

"What did he want?"

"I know you'll be shocked to learn that the reverend has enemies. Someone's been posting unflattering parodies on You-Tube."

"I want to see them."

We went into my office and looked up Angel of Truth. Sure enough, there were several videos featuring a man dressed in a suit and wearing a blond wig and lots of makeup running around flapping a Bible and screaming that everyone was going to hell and mangling Bible verses so they were incomprehensible. In one video, the phony preacher foamed at the mouth so much, a team of carpet cleaners wearing gas masks had to come in and vacuum around the pulpit and down the aisle of the church. I thought the videos were pretty funny, but Camden didn't think so.

"Ingram said he'd recently fired a man named Eric O'Connor."

"Did he say why?"

"Said he was fishy and weird."

"Takes one to know one."

"Amen, brother."

I clicked back to the Angel of Truth's YouTube page. He or she had several videos listed. All of them featured what the Angel called *The Bibilicious Hour*. I watched a few more, but Camden sat down in the chair across from my desk where he couldn't see the screen.

"These are pretty ridiculous," I said. "All he'd have to do is laugh them off."

"I don't think he knows how to laugh," Camden said.

"Is Kary all right?" I asked.

"She was a little shaken up, but she went on to school. It was a shock for her to hear the man's voice after all this time."

"I can't believe that guy's her father."

"I can't believe you're going to help him."

"Kary asked me to. She's turning the other cheek." I clicked off YouTube and went to my phone directory program. There were two Eric O'Conners listed. The first one I called said he had never worked at the church. He sounded like an elderly man, so I didn't think he was the Eric I wanted. When I called the second O'Conner, there was no answer, and no voice mail. His address was listed as 456 Edgewood Drive. He would have to wait until I confirmed this address with the church. "Sure you're not up for a little trip down Freedom's Path?"

"Don't you mean Freedom Path United Church of the Revelation?"

"Yeah, Pastor Gary didn't like my use of the short form."

"He's head of a vast conglomeration that preaches hellfire and damnation, scaring his congregations into loving Jesus, and sucking every last penny out of the hands of the poor and the deluded. That's insane. That's why people don't want to be Christians. They see that on TV and run the other way."

"That was one of his first questions. Was I a Christian?"

"I hope you said no, not your kind of Christian."

"I'm not any kind of Christian. That's your department. But he promised to convert me if I solved his case."

This made Camden grin. "I'd like to see him try."

***

After Camden left, I sat at my desk and surveyed my surroundings. Nice neat desk, computer, printer, phone with answering machine. A bookshelf with a few plants on top, clean sheer curtains at the wide front window giving me an unobstructed view of the porch, the front yard with its large oak trees, and quiet Grace Street. Upstairs, on the second floor at the back, was my bedroom, a large comfortable green room with plenty of light, a bedroom I shared with Kary. It was, as I'd said, ideal.

But soon there'd be the baby. Camden would need help. He'd never been a father before, and as I knew, raising a child was one crisis after another. I didn't have to be psychic to know Ellin would be too busy with her job and would leave the child care to him. But what about me? Would the sight of another baby girl reduce me to a blubbering mess?

Now what brought that on?

I glanced at my calendar. Maybe part of the problem was January 20, only a couple of weeks away. January 20, heavy with significance, the date leaping off the page to smack me in the heart.

Lindsey's birthday. She had died in a car accident not long after her eighth birthday, four years ago.

But she wasn't gone, as she kept reminding me. I could almost hear her stern little voice telling me to stop wallowing and keep moving forward.

In fact, I did hear her voice. Even though she was safe in her heavenly playground, Lindsey had found a way to communicate with me in my dreams, and more recently, during the day.

Just as she did now.

That's right, Daddy, she said. *I know my birthday's coming, and you shouldn't be sad. There's someone else you need to help.*

Once Lindsey had A Cause, I had no choice but to solve the mystery. David Randall, Detective to the Dead.

"Okay, baby," I said. "Who's the person who needs my help?"

The sad lady.

Here's where things got tricky. Sometimes I knew exactly who Lindsey meant, living or dead. Sometimes, Lindsey would make it possible for a spirit who needed my help to talk to me. And sometimes, like today, Lindsey's reference was an obscure clue I had to figure out.

"Can you tell me more about this sad lady?" I asked.

You'll know.

Her voice faded. That was all I was going to get for now.

For a long time I couldn't even bear the thought of seeing Lindsey's picture. No more of that. I had her picture where I could see it, right there on my desk in a silver frame. Her second grade school picture. She wore her white lace dress, her long brown curls held back with a white ribbon. She'd taken one of her favorite stuffed animals to school and had her picture made holding the fuzzy black kitten and beaming, knowing everyone would be surprised when she brought the pictures home. I imagined the smile on the photographer's face, too. I laughed when I saw the picture for the first time.

Now I smiled every time I looked at it, knowing she was still with me.

***

Freedom Path United Church of the Revelation was not a church. It was a village. The sprawling complex of buildings took up an entire block out near the airport. I drove my white '67 Plymouth Fury around twice before I spotted the largest structure in the village, a huge white stone church with a steeple and a bell tower. A sign on the church grounds said "Sanctuary and Main Office." I parked the Fury and walked up the sidewalk to a set of large double doors carved with flowers and vines. As I entered, chimes rang out and echoed down a silvery hallway where ceiling high windows let in muted sunlight. Huge vases filled with real flowers stood on a marble-topped table where an array of carefully arranged pamphlets and brochures trumpeted the church's many programs: Sunday School, couples counseling, community outreach, soup kitchen, after-school tutoring, AA meetings, even Yoga classes.

"May I help you?" a soft voice asked.

I turned. An older man smiled at me. He was conservatively dressed in khaki slacks, white shirt, and a black tie. He looked about fifty, his graying hair neatly combed, and his brown eyes shining behind gold framed glasses.

"David Randall. I met with Pastor Ingram earlier, and he invited me to have a look around."

"We're delighted to have you, Mr. Randall. I'm Carl, a member of the Welcome Committee. Please let me give you a tour."

Carl kept his voice low and soothing as we walked past a large office area. People manned computer stations, answering phones and typing away. I heard soft music playing but didn't recognize the hymn. "I Surrender All," most likely.

Carl pointed out the various departments. "Here's where anyone can call with a problem or a question and get an immediate answer," he said. "Our finance officers take care of the tithes we receive. Over here we have our Bible specialists who are on hand to give clear concise interpretations of the Word. And here are our scheduling officers who revise the calendar and keep everyone up to date on the many events that happen at the church."

"Where does Eric O'Connor work?" I asked.

Carl's helpful face looked regretful. "I'm sorry. Eric no longer works for us."

"Uh, oh," I said. "I was afraid this might happen. Eric has trouble keeping a job."

"Oh, he was a good worker," Carl said. "I'm afraid his ideas for the future of the church and ours did not mesh. You see, Pastor Ingram has definite plans for Freedom Path United Church of the Revelation, and everyone who works here needs to be in sync with that plan."

"So Eric was on the board or the planning committee?"

"Dear me, no. He worked in our outreach office, calling folks and inviting them to our services." There was a slight tic in Carl's eye. "We have a prepared speech for our outreach employees to make certain they cover everything the church offers. I'm afraid Eric got a little creative with the message. A fine young man, but not a team player."

So everything was fine unless you deviated from Pastor Gary's master plan. Sounded like there was a little more to Eric. "I understand," I said.

Carl motioned me forward. "Let me show you our Story Garden."

We walked out of the office area and through another set of carved double doors that led to a garden. No doubt in the spring it was a masterpiece, but in winter it looked bare and gray, except for the shiny white marble statues, which, as far as I could tell, depicted various scenes from the Bible.

Carl gestured, his eyes gleaming with pride. "It's a little bleak in January, of course. You'll have to come see it when everything's in full bloom. Here's John the Baptist baptizing Our Lord, and over here is the Good Samaritan." He cocked an ear to the music wafting out of the bell tower. "Oh, that's 'In the Garden.' How appropriate. I believe that's my favorite hymn. Do you have a favorite hymn, Mr. Randall?"

I searched my memory and fortunately recalled the Lutheran theme song. "'A Mighty Fortress.'"

"An excellent hymn. I'll have to ask our choir to sing that one for our next service. The old hymns are the best. Everything you need to know about God and His love can be found in those wonderful songs."

"Amen," I said.

"In the Garden" wasn't Carl's only favorite hymn. As we toured the Story Garden, he told me all about the history of many more. When he stopped for breath, I decided it was time to get to the point. "As one of Pastor Ingram's secretaries, I'm sure you are aware there are some very unflattering videos of Pastor Ingram on the Internet?"

This didn't shake his serenity. "We're aware. We've gotten several calls about this."

"Pastor Ingram asked me to find out who's behind them. Do you have any idea?"

"Aside from the Devil?"

I could hear the capital "D." "You really believe the devil's been posting those videos?"

He smiled at me in the patient way of a parent with a small child. "Mr. Randall, it is a known fact that the Devil is alive and well and working his evil ways. I'm sure he has no problem finding poor Godless souls to do his dirty work on Earth. Someone as wise and holy as Pastor Ingram is a very attractive target for Satan.

But the harder he tries, the harder we will fight back."

"Let's say for some horrible reason, the Internet Devil wins, and the church goes under. Who would benefit?"

"You'd have to ask Pastor Ingram. But the Devil will never win."

"Is he in? The pastor, I mean, not the devil."

Carl's face still had the same calm expression. "He's in a very important meeting this afternoon, sir." Another hymn began to play and his face lit up. "'Onward Christian Soldiers'! One of my favorites."

I let Carl show me the vast golden sanctuary and the smaller chapel with its dazzling stained glass windows. I thanked him for the tour and the information. He showed me the secretary's office where I checked the contact information for Eric O'Conner. 456 Edgewood Drive, the same address I'd found. Enough overblown religion. Time to seek out the Angel of Truth.

CHAPTER THREE

"War of the Worlds"

After I left the church, I gave Eric O'Conner another call. No answer. I drove to 456 Edgewood Drive to see if he was home. The house was a dingy green color with a saggy front porch and uneven blinds dangling in the windows. There wasn't a car in the driveway, but I got out and knocked on the front door. There was no answer. I peered past the crooked blinds, but I couldn't see anything except dim shadows of what looked like a sofa and chair. I walked around past overflowing trash cans, a rusty grill, and a chipped and faded garden gnome to the equally unappealing back of the house. The whole place looked abandoned. If Eric O'Conner was the Angel of Truth, maybe he'd found another hideout or skipped town to avoid the wrath of Pastor Ingram.

When I got back to 302 Grace, it was almost three o'clock. Camden was in the back hallway, working on the washing machine, which had decided to leak. It's a good thing he's handy, or costs for repairs on the house would be astronomical.

"How's Kary?" I asked. He would know if anything was wrong.

He pulled out the washer's filter and put it back in again. He must have fixed it because it slid in smoothly. "Stop fretting. You find out anything at the church?"

"The Story Garden's nice, and Eric O'Conner's still not home.

The devil must have got him, and speaking of the devil, it's after three. You're supposed to be at the Psychic Network."

"Damn."

He changed out of his jeans and tee shirt into the clothes he wears when he works at Tamara's Boutique: light blue shirt, dark slacks, and the blue tie my mother gave him for Christmas. I revved up the Fury and drove us to the TV studio where the Psychic Service Network broadcast its shows.

I swung the car into a parking place near the front of the red brick building. "Here we are. Snyders, beware!"

Camden unhooked his seat belt. "I think I'll tell the Snyder boys, no, I'm not psychic, never have been. I don't know where Ellie gets these ideas."

We went inside and were instantly accosted by Reg Haverson. Reg was tall and preppy, the kind of man who gets his teeth professionally flossed. He had dreams of taking over the network and was always coming up with peculiar and impractical ideas. For the PSN, this is saying a lot.

"Guys, which one of these do you like best? A Psychic Sweepstakes to win a session with the psychic of your choice, a Psychic Bake-off to see who can conjure up the most out of this world cake, or my favorite, a Miss Paranormal pageant! Wouldn't it be fantastic?"

Camden tried to talk him down from this particular ledge. "Reg, I don't think Ellie would go for any of those."

"So? She never likes my ideas. The telethon I wanted to do would've been great. I had everything lined up. Then she shot down my crop-circle contest for 'New Age News,' which would have been a solid ratings getter. But these are different. Everyone loves a sweepstakes, everyone loves cake, and I know a pageant would be dynamite."

Yes, there were bound to be some explosions.

Ignoring Camden's frown that said, don't encourage him, I said, "I think a Psychic Bake-Off sounds like fun. Bermuda Triangle Brownies, Ouija Board Pie."

Reg didn't want to let go of his favorite idea. "I've already got people interested in that, and at least three women interested in a pageant." Reg reached in his suit pocket and pulled out his cell phone to check his list. "A Miss Tarot Card, a Miss Astral Projection, and one young lady hasn't decided, but I'm thinking she'll make a great Miss Séance."

"Reg, I hate to tell you, but you're wasting your time," Camden said.

"Do you actually know this?" Reg asked. "I mean, 'know' it, as in seeing my future?"

"I know this on all levels."

Reg hesitated for only a second. "Well. We'll see about that." He straightened his tie and hurried off.

"He never learns, does he?" I said.

"Your insight is as accurate as mine."

Camden and I said hello to Teresa Perello, one of the women who hosted PSN programs. She looked lovely as usual in her flowing psychic dress. I asked her where the Deadly Duo might be lurking.

"You mean Sean and Geoff? They aren't so bad. Geoff's a little full of himself, but I can live with that." She readjusted the microphone on the collar of her dress, gold bracelets jangling. "Cam, you look very handsome."

"Thank you," he said. "Let's get this over with."

Teresa took his arm and led him toward the set, a sofa and chairs in muted New Age tones of pink and beige and a flower arrangement surrounded by large crystals. "Now, now. You know you look good on TV."

Sean and Geoff were already seated on the sofa. They were brothers, but you'd never know it. Sean was short and dark with a pained expression. Geoff was tall, with a lot of wavy red hair and a fierce smile. I'd seen them on talk shows and morning shows, dismissing the claims of famous psychics and revealing their secret techniques. Ellin had met them at a broadcasters convention in nearby Charlotte, and when they found out her husband was psychic, they insisted on meeting him. So far, Camden had managed to avoid them. They greeted Camden and shook hands all around.

That's good, I thought. You just gave him all the information he needs to know.

Camden sat down in one chair; Teresa took the other. I noticed Camden looked unsettled, but he hated talking about his talent, especially on camera. In the background, Ellin signaled for the taping to begin. Teresa turned her bright smile to the audience.

"Good afternoon and welcome to *Ready to Believe*. Our special guests today are Sean and Geoff Snyder, exposers of the paranormal, and Camden, one of Parkland's most gifted psychics. Good afternoon, gentlemen."

"Good afternoon," they said.

"Let's start with you, Sean. You and your brother are the authors of three successful books, *Take Charge of Your Own Destiny, Secrets of So-Called Psychics*, and *Don't Be A Dupe*. Would you comment on your findings?"

Sean leaned forward. "Teresa, I'm happy to say we've had great success in uncovering the duplicity of these people who say they're psychic, when really they're con artists, preying on the gullible and those fearful of the future."

"Exactly how do you do this?"

"By confronting the people directly, by forcing them to display their powers, which of course, they can't do."

"Camden, would you like to respond?"

Camden looked as if he'd like to be anywhere but there and, as usual, downplayed his many psychic abilities "I was born with a certain talent to see past and future events. I've tried to be useful, to help people when they ask me, but I don't go around displaying my powers, such as they are."

Geoff looked smug. "Perhaps you could give us a demonstration?"

"I don't think so."

"Because you can't."

"Because you wouldn't like what I'd tell you."

Geoff grinned. "Ohh, I'm scared now. Is one of us going to die?"

Camden didn't answer right away. He looked from Geoff's self-satisfied smirk to Sean. Uh-ho, I thought. He's seen something unfortunate in Sean's immediate future.

"It's not something I'd care to discuss on the air."

"Well, what can you discuss on the air?" Geoff asked. "Perhaps you could tell us about the tall dark stranger, or the gold hidden under the staircase."

"I can tell you I've helped some people in the past. One man took my advice and survived a plane crash."

"Which he might have done anyway."

Camden paused as if to give this statement the benefit of the doubt. "One young woman was able to deal with the death of her child."

"Which any qualified psychiatrist would have been able to handle. What about those so-called abductees you're associated with? Do these people actually believe they've been taken by aliens?"

I tried to catch Ellin's eye. Lily Wilkes, Camden's neighbor, occasionally asked for his help with her alien abductees support group. Who told the Snyders about this, I wonder? Ellin ignored me.

"I try to help those people understand their experiences," Camden said.

"Which are totally false."

"Which are very real to them."

"I still think you need to give me and Sean a reading. Or do you need some sort of props? Tarot cards, maybe, or a crystal ball?"

You have to push Camden a lot to get him angry, but once he's mad, it can get dangerous. His eyes got dark and he set his mouth in a firm line. The crystals on the table began to twitch.

Hold it together, Camden, I thought, hoping he'd hear me. Ellin had been thrilled by his last display of telekinesis on her show when he'd been high on headache medicine—long story—and a return performance of this talent would doom him forever.

Geoff didn't notice the crystals. He leaned over to his brother. "It's always the same, isn't it, Sean? These people spout off all kinds of ephemeral advice, but when it comes to facts, they can't deliver."

"Here are a couple of facts," Camden said. "You, Geoff, wanted to be a ballet dancer, but your father forbade it, so you ran away from home. You haven't spoken to anyone else in your family in twenty-five years, and it's killing you. You're famous, your books sell well, but this means nothing without your father's approval. You haven't told Sean about it, but you're thinking of writing another book, a book about your dream to be a dancer. It colors all your thoughts. You want to call this book *My Lost Dance*."

Geoff Snyder went white and sat back.

"Geoff?" Sean said. "Is this true?"

"Oh, my lord," Ellin said.

Camden turned to Sean. "As for you, you're still mourning the death of your wife, even though you were less than kind to her."

Sean Snyder gasped. "Stop it."

"More than anything, you wish she were still alive, so you could apologize, and try to do better."

"You couldn't know that—someone told you—"

"No one told me. When we shook hands, it leaped into my mind. It might as well have been written in letters of fire. You see what these 'powers' can do? You see why I don't come on shows like this?" He turned to Geoff. "Anything else you want to know?"

Geoff shook his head. Teresa, who'd be staring, open-mouthed, now got control and gave the camera another bright smile. "And now a word from our sponsors, Kitty Kare Kat Food and Lunch in a Can."

CHAPTER FOUR

"Two Lost Worlds"

As soon as Ellin signaled all clear, Camden got up and walked off the set. The flower arrangement fell over, and the crystals rolled in all directions. Teresa thought he'd bumped the table. Geoff and Sean remained seated, stunned.

Camden came to me, his eyes still smoldering.

"Nice shootin,' Tex," I said. "Got a round left for the missus?"

Ellin advanced. I braced for the explosion. Instead, she grabbed Camden and kissed him like they were the only two survivors of a ten-car crash.

"You were wonderful! What a show! Our ratings will go through the roof!"

Leave it to Ellin to care first and foremost for her show.

Camden pulled away. "No, I wasn't wonderful, Ellie. I let my temper get the best of me."

"I loved it! You put those two in their place."

He gestured to the audience, leaning over to hear every word. "By exposing their innermost secrets to all these people?"

"That's what Sean and Geoff wanted to do to you."

"Well, it was unfair. They were unarmed."

"Don't be silly."

"Ellie." He took hold of her arms to get her attention. "Something's going to happen to Sean."

Ellin stared, and I said, "What?"

"Unless he takes precautions, he's going to die later tonight. That's what really threw me at the beginning."

"You'd better warn him," I said.

Camden glanced back at the set. The Snyder brothers were in earnest conversation with each other. "Think they'll believe me?"

"Yeah, if they're smart."

But Sean and Geoff wanted nothing more to do with him.

"You've said more than enough," Geoff said.

Camden wasn't going to leave without warning Sean. "Sean, tonight, at your hotel, be careful. Don't go anywhere alone. I see something very dangerous and possibly tragic in your future. If you stay with Geoff, you should be all right."

Sean stared at him. "There's no way you could've known about Natalie."

As usual, Camden felt guilty about his outburst. "If it's any consolation, your wife loved you until the day she died. She still loves you."

Sean's mouth trembled and he blinked away sudden tears. Geoff took his arm and pulled him away. "That's enough."

Ellin looked disappointed. "Now why didn't we get that on camera?"

Even though I know this woman, sometimes I can't believe her. "You are a ghoul. You should work for the *Inquirer*."

"Ten seconds," someone called.

"Camden," she said.

He shook his head. "I've done enough damage. They can talk to Teresa now. Come on, Randall."

Ellin packed a lot of complaining into those remaining seconds, but Camden stood firm. Finally, she gave up and signaled to Teresa, who had straightened the set, to continue the interview without him. I knew this wouldn't throw Teresa, and the Snyders seemed relieved.

We went out and got into the Fury. Camden slumped in his seat. "I'll never hear the end of this."

"Are you sure about something bad happening to Sean?" I asked. "It's not just wishful thinking?"

"When we first shook hands, I felt a very strong premonition of death."

"Maybe you were seeing his wife's death."

"Maybe."

"What did you mean, 'less than kind'?"

He loosened his tie. "He abused her, but I wasn't going to say that on TV."

"That wormy guy? He doesn't look like the type."

"He hit her several times. It made him feel like a big man."

I've known Camden for almost ten years, and this kind of thing still amazed me. "You got all that from the handshake."

"Most of it radiates from him in black waves." He gave me a wry grin. "That's the scientific explanation."

"Well, you've got them good and spooked and almost impaled."

"I saw the crystals moving and tried to calm down."

"Is it under control?"

"Almost." He glanced back toward the studio. "I suppose it's too much to hope Ellie will leave me alone now."

"Are you kidding? That's exactly the kind of thing she wants you to do. She's probably got lots of guests lined up for target practice. Who knows what hideous secrets you can divulge?"

"Why can't she understand I don't want to divulge secrets, hideous, or otherwise?" He paused. "'Divulge'? That's impressive."

"That's nothing. I used sanctimonious earlier today."

"For Pastor Ingram, no doubt."

"A master of hypocritical piety. That's two more right there. You are falling so far behind in the vocabulary challenge."

"Then I'd better have a milkshake to restore my powers."

***

We went home by way of the Quik-Fry so Camden could get his milkshake and settle down. It was after five o'clock, and Kary was already home. I always like to greet her and have a Diet Coke ready. I wished I'd been home in time to greet her.

Camden decided that even though it was chilly outside, he

wanted to sit on the porch swing to finish his milkshake. I knew he was still processing all the Snyder thoughts.

I thought Kary might be sitting at the piano playing something sad, but she was in the kitchen fixing supper. She insisted on taking her turn each week. Once Camden and I got up the nerve to tell her that her tuna casserole was less than palatable, she started trying other recipes with varying degrees of success. A can of tomato soup, a box of macaroni and cheese, and a package of frozen fish sticks were lined up on the counter next to the stove. I wasn't sure how this was going to turn out.

She turned from the stove to greet me. "Hi, David. Have any luck?"

"More to the point, how are you doing?"

"Oh, I'm fine. It was a shock at first, hearing that voice, but he's not a part of my life, and I don't want him to be, so as soon as you solve his problem, we don't ever have to mention him again." She paused in the act of opening a cabinet. "What is the problem, anyway?"

"Someone calling himself or herself the Angel of Truth has made and posted some absurd videos making fun of the pastor and his preaching style."

"Is that all? Why is he so upset? Oh, I should've remembered. He never could take a joke."

I sat down at the counter that separated the kitchen from the dining room and moved Kary's textbooks, *Elements and Essential Strategies of Guidance, The School Counselor's Guide to Helping Students With Anger Management Issues, Implementing Restorative Practices in Schools*—just a little light reading. I set the grocery frog, a frog-shaped planter that held all our loose change, on top of the stack. "I need to get online and check out the local Christian chat rooms to see what people have to say about Pastor Gary. He could think of only one person who he's had a conflict with. Recently. Eric O'Conner. Ever hear of him?"

She took a glass baking dish out of the cabinet and shut the door. "No, but I've been away from that church for years."

"The church on steroids."

"Yes, isn't it ostentatious?"

"'Ostentatious.' Twenty points."

"Come on, that's at least twenty-five," she said.

"Yes, it's huge and showy and full of happy drones, any one of whom could be leading a double life as Satan's little helper. I did learn a lot about hymns from the man who gave me the tour, though."

Kary wrestled a large spoon out of the silverware drawer. "Is Carl still there? Oh, yes, he can go on and on about hymns. He was always very nice to me."

"Do you have a favorite hymn?"

"I'd have to think about that." She came and sat across from me."David, I don't want you to waste your time on this. So what if someone's making fun of my father on the Internet? Everyone makes fun of people on the Internet. It's not going to impact his income, is it? People might come to Freedom Path to see what he's really like. If that's all it is, I say forget it. He can get God to smite the bad guy." She started to get up.

"He paid me."

She sat back down. "What? Actual money?"

I dug the check out of my billfold. "See?"

She took the check and stared at it, mystified. "I wonder what he's really worried about."

"Maybe he's afraid the videos are going to reveal some dark secret he's hiding. Cheating on your mom, maybe? That seems to be the m.o. of most televangelists."

"Ugh. I don't even want to think about that." Kary handed the check back to me. "Let's talk about something else. Something pleasant, like the baby on the way." Her expression changed. "Or is that going to be too hard?"

"What's so hard? It's a baby, that's all."

"A baby that will probably bring up all sorts of memories for you."

"I can look at a baby, for goodness sake. I can handle it. You'll have sad memories, too, won't you?"

"But I never even got to hold mine."

I never even got to hold mine. Every time I think I've got it bad, I'm reminded that Kary went through the same tragedy, and I could kick myself for wallowing in my own self-pity. Was Kary the sad lady Lindsey wanted me to help?

Kary cleared her throat and wiped her eyes. "So I'm looking forward to having a baby in the house."

I reached across the counter and took her hands in mine. "We'll handle it together."

***

While dinner cooked or baked or evolved, I went online and looked up the local Christian websites and visited a few chat rooms. Most of them deplored Pastor Gary's over-the-top preaching style, but admitted his church was doing a lot of good work in Parkland. One site called "A Light in the Darkness" mentioned the parody videos and encouraged followers to watch them. Comments indicated everyone was having a laugh at Pastor Gary's expense, but there were no threats against him personally. I browsed back a couple of years into the archives, but found nothing.

It wasn't long before the smell of fish told me dinner was ready. This particular casserole was runny in places where it should have been solid, but fortunately, there were always crackers. I slipped extra bits of macaroni-covered fish down to Cindy, our gray house-cat, and her black and white kitten, Oreo. They had learned that under my chair was always a good place to score snacks.

Kary could always tell when Camden wasn't one hundred percent, so he explained about the Snyders.

"Of course they wouldn't listen to your warnings," she said.

"No. I'd already told them too much, so I pretty well screwed up there."

"But it sounds like they provoked you."

I reached for the crackers. "You should've seen him. It was Evil Camden, all fire and brimstone."

"They must have really riled you, Cam."

"Lightning shooting out of his eyes. Objects poised for flight."

"I've seen it and it's quite impressive. More casserole, guys?"

Camden waved the dish away. "No, thanks. I'm not too hungry tonight."

Using his burst of power as an excuse. Nice. "I'll take a little more, Kary." Bonus points for me. I kept my smile as she plopped another spoonful onto my plate. "Thanks."

"More for you, Stuart?"

Stuart had managed to wedge the remaining chunk of his portion into an impressive little cracker fort. "I've had plenty. Don't forget we've got cake for dessert. Let me get it."

Stuart had brought home an unwanted birthday cake from Super Food. The decorator in the bakery department thought the customer said "boot" when she really said "boat." As a result of the mistake, we were now the proud owners of a large blue boot-shaped cake trimmed in white with white icing boot laces that spelled "Happy Birthday, Barry."

Stuart set the cake down in the middle of the table. "I call the toe."

Camden cut a piece from the top of the boot that included a generous portion of icing. He slid it onto his plate and paused, gazing thoughtfully at Kary.

"What?" she said.

"I don't know," he said. "I got an odd little family vibe."

"Well, I'm slightly annoyed at my old family, as you may have noticed." She took the cake knife and sliced a small piece of cake from the boot's heel. "But I have you guys as my family now."

"Yes, and I'm very happy about that."

"Then it was a good vibe, right?" I said. "Enjoy the good vibes while they last."

"It must have something to do with the baby," Kary said. "We're adding to our family, and I can't wait to see her."

We were almost finished by the time Ellin came home. She was still so pleased by the show, she practically danced into the house, and since Ellin can't dance, this was a scary sight.

"That was amazing, Cam! Viewers are going to go crazy over you. You have to come back."

"To ruin someone else's day? No, thank you."

"The rest of the program went fine."

"You mean the Snyders shook off Camden's revelations and continued snyding away?" I asked.

"Teresa got them to talk about their plans for their presentation at ExtravaganzaCon. They were fine, I'm telling you."

Camden was still concerned about Sean's future. "Did they say anything afterwards about taking precautions tonight?"

"I didn't get another chance to speak to them. They left right after the program. Cam, I've got another super skeptic lined up for next week. He is amazingly pompous. One little handshake, and I'll bet you could deflate him."

She'd known him for years, married him, was carrying his child, and she still didn't have a clue how he operated. I gave Camden my best I Told You So look, which he ignored.

"Ellie, I'm not going to do that kind of thing."

"But I don't understand. It's so easy for you."

"That's why it's so dangerous." He put his arms around her and pulled her close. "I've been through this, a long time ago, when I was a different person, a person I never want to be again. You don't have to understand, just please drop this whole thing."

She started to say something when Camden said, "Oh!"

"What? What is it?"

"The baby," he said in wonder. "I think I heard her."

"Sweetie, that's impossible. She's only five months old."

He kept her in his embrace. "No, she tried to say something. I'm sure it was the baby."

"She probably wants some coffee," I said.

Camden kissed Ellin. "You need to get off your feet."

"Think you can carry me, big boy?"

"If that's what it takes."

"We haven't finished our discussion."

He picked her up. "We'll finish upstairs."

Since most of their disagreements ended upstairs, I was surprised Camden didn't pick more fights with her. The boot cake tasted better than it looked, and after we cleaned up the kitchen, Kary graded papers until she needed to get to bed.

"I'll be up in a minute," I said.

Cindy sat in my lap while I continued my search of Christian websites. Then I called my reliable sources, hoping one of them might have information about Eric O'Conner, but they didn't. I'm not that fond of cats, but Cindy always seemed to know when I'd like company, so even with her tail in my face, I managed to get my work done by ten. When I went up to my bedroom, Cindy followed and hopped up on the bed where she curled around Kary.

"Back off," I said. "That's my job."

Kary yawned and shifted position so that Cindy had to move. I thought she went back to sleep, but when I'd had my shower and slid in next to her, she smiled and gave me a kiss.

I put my arm around her and pulled her close. "Your mac and fish was good."

"Liar. I saw how many crackers you ate."

"I needed a little extra crunch."

"Here's your extra crunch." She punched my shoulder, which led to a wrestling match that I won.

Afterwards, I lay awake a while, thinking about Pastor Ingram and how I'd like to kick him in his fat pew-sitting rear until he bounced down the aisle of the church and landed head first in the baptismal font. I imagined the look on his face if I told him I was sleeping with his daughter and planned to spend my life with her— not that I needed or wanted his blessing. I decided after I solved his case, I'd tell him I was a full-on follower of Satan who led the Black Sabbath services every night down by the junkyard.

With these kinds of thoughts, it was no wonder I dreamed about a huge congregation of animal-headed people with horns and pitchforks who cheered as I gave them baskets of kittens and puppies and then, as Pastor Ingram tried to shout them down, began stomping their feet louder and louder until I woke with a start.

CHAPTER FIVE

"The Invisible Monster"

The stomping was a furious pounding on our front door. Kary sat up, pushing back her tangled hair. "What in the world?"

A quick glance at my alarm clock showed it was eleven thirty. I got downstairs before Camden, which was lucky, because I opened the door on a distraught and panting Geoff Snyder.

"Where is he? Tell me where he is! He did this to me! He killed Sean!"

I tried to get him to settle down and come into my office, but he struck at me and pushed me away. Kary had followed me, and then Camden and Ellin came halfway down the stairs and paused. Geoff pointed a trembling finger at Camden.

"You knew it was going to happen! You must have had something to do with it. You killed him."

"What the hell are you talking about?" Ellin said. "Randall, get that lunatic out of the house."

"What's all the racket?" came Stuart's voice.

"It's okay," I said.

"'Okay'?" Geoff Snyder's face was a mask of rage. "How can you say that? My brother is dead!"

Camden remained calm. "Why didn't you stay with him?"

I knew the answer to that one. Despite everything Camden had told the Snyders during *Ready to Believe*, they still refused to believe.

"He went downstairs to the lobby for a newspaper." Suddenly Geoff broke down and began to sob. "Did you see the murderer? Did you see who did this? Can you find them?"

"Come on." I led him into the island and sat him down on the sofa.

Camden followed and offered him the box of tissues from the table. "Geoff, I'm very sorry this happened. I wish I could tell you more. I can't control what I see and what I don't see. Images just flash into my mind."

"Will you help me? Help me find the murderer?"

"I'll do what I can, but Randall's a private eye."

Geoff raised his head. Tears streamed down his face. "Would you be willing to take this case?"

"Yes, of course," I said. "Tell me everything you can."

Geoff wiped his face. "After the show, we went back to my room at the hotel. Naturally, we were a bit rattled by what Camden had said, so I told Sean to stay in my room. We had a couple of drinks and I took a nap. This was around six, I think, and I slept about an hour. When I woke up, Sean was watching TV. He said, let's have room service, so we ordered some food, and after we ate, I said I was going to work on our next book, and he said—" He paused for control. "—he said, why don't you start *My Lost Dance?*" He stared at Camden in wonder. "I haven't told a living soul about that book, not even Sean."

"I saw it shining in front of you," Camden said.

Geoff swallowed hard. "We talked for quite a while about my plans, and then Sean said he was going downstairs to get a paper."

"When was this?"

"About ten o'clock. After thirty minutes, he wasn't back, so I went to look for him. When I got to the lobby, all hell had broken loose. A member of the housekeeping staff had found him in the stairwell and called the ambulance and the police. He was already dead. He'd been stabbed." His voice quit. He took a drink and wiped his face again. "Nobody saw anything. Sean was in the wrong place at the wrong time."

I didn't say it, but I knew we were all thinking if the Snyder brothers had listened to Camden's warning there wouldn't have been a wrong place or a wrong time.

Kary went to Geoff, offering condolences, and patted his hand as he began to sob again. Ellin said she'd make some coffee. Stuart said he'd help. After a while, Geoff took a deep breath and apologized for bursting in and waking everyone.

I was concerned that Geoff had left the scene of the crime. "Have the police already talked to you?" I asked.

"No, they told me to wait. By then, it was after eleven, and I couldn't stand it anymore. I had to do something, so when they were talking to the hotel staff, I slipped out, but I—I wasn't thinking. I know they suspect me, but Camden had seen the murder. I knew where Ellin lived—I had to do something."

"Right now, everyone's a suspect," I said. "You should go back right away and cooperate fully."

"I'll come, too," Camden said.

Geoff started out and froze at the door. "There's a police car out there. They followed me!"

I took a look. "Take it easy." To Camden, I said, "It's Jordan."

I opened the door and let Jordan Finley in. He stood for a moment, his large square shape filling the doorway, his sharp blue eyes taking in the scene of Geoff cowering in the foyer next to Camden. Then he rubbed his short stiff black hair.

"I might have known. What's the connection this time, Cam?"

"I saw Sean's death earlier today. Unfortunately, he didn't believe me."

Jordan's sharp gaze pinpointed Geoff. "Mr. Snyder comes running to you? For what?"

Geoff was shaking. "I wasn't running. I didn't do anything."

"You took off from the hotel like you were on fire," Jordan said. "That wasn't very smart."

"I had to get to Camden. I had to talk to him."

"We would've been glad to get him for you. Or you could've called."

Geoff shook his head. "I wasn't thinking. Sean's dead. Camden saw it happen. I don't know what I thought."

"I was going to bring Geoff back to the hotel," I told Jordan.

Ellin had been quiet long enough. "He came bursting in here like a madman."

"I'm very sorry, Mrs. Camden."

"Jordan, I'd like to come have a look," Camden said.

Jordan thought it over. He hated having me involved in his business, but usually when our paths crossed we ended up sharing information, with Jordan taking most of the credit. Camden was another story. He'd helped Jordan find murderers and missing people, and he'd been a big help tracking down a serial killer this past November. Jordan was willing to go along with psychic assistance, but he wanted as little publicity about it as possible.

"Let my people finish, and you can have a look." He pointed to Geoff. "Mr. Snyder, it would be a good idea if you came down to the station of your own free will right now, and you," the finger swung to me, "you'll stay out of this."

"Mr. Snyder's hired me to find Sean's killer."

Jordan glared. "Great."

Geoff held his ground. "That's true. I want Randall on this case, and Camden, too."

"Randall will only get in the way."

"I don't care. I want the killer found and brought to justice. I don't care how many people I have to hire." He stomped out the door.

Jordan motioned for one of his officers to follow Geoff. He turned back to me and shook his head, exasperated. "Honest to God, Randall. Why does this keep happening?"

"If he and Sean had listened to Camden, we wouldn't be standing here now."

"He was furious," Ellin said. "He accused Cam of murdering his brother."

"What exactly did you see?" Jordan asked Camden.

"Sean in a stairwell, stabbed to death."

Jordan let his breath out in a long "Whew. That's where we found him, and that's how he died. Get dressed and come on over to the hotel. I'll let you in as soon as my team gives the okay."

"The Parkland Hilton?" I said, displaying a previously unknown clairvoyance.

"What of it?" said Jordan.

"Site of the amazing, star-studded ExtravaganzaCon. Geoff and Sean were scheduled to speak at the Con. We're going to have a galaxy full of suspects."

Camden and I exchanged ominous glances, then went upstairs to change.

***

Jordan didn't want me contaminating the scene of the crime, so when he took Camden to the stairwell, he ordered me to stay in the lobby. Fair enough. I'd done some work for the Parkland Hilton in the past, so the manager let me talk to the desk clerk and the housekeeper who'd found Sean. The clerk was a skinny young man of about twenty-five, wide-eyed at the thought of murder in his hotel and, seeing as how I'd made my entrance along with a phalanx of cops, he was more than willing to tell all.

"It was about ten o'clock when Lupe came screaming in, saying somebody was dead in the stairwell. She said, 'Call an ambulance, call the police,' so I did right away."

"Did you see the body?"

"No, I had to stay at the desk and tell the police and everybody where to go when they got here. When they identified the man, I tried calling his room, then his brother appeared, looking for him."

"Which stairwell was it?"

"North stairs. Between the seventh and eighth floors."

"Are the elevators at the north end all working?

"Yes."

"Which floor were the Snyders on?"

"Eighth. Why would he want to walk down eight floors?"

"Exercise? Or a secret rendezvous?"

The clerk shuddered. "That's a creepy thought. I sure hope this doesn't hurt the convention. We've had several people check out already because of this."

"The SF paranormal crowd is pretty tough. And this convention is a big event."

"Don't I know it. We've had to take on extra help to staff the hospitality rooms. We're booked solid and expecting over five hundred walk-ins in the morning."

Housekeeper Lupe was small and round, her shiny black hair scraped back in a tight ponytail. She was insulted by the clerk's description. "I never came screaming up to the desk. Why would I alarm everyone like that? I was upset, of course, but I asked very calmly for him to call for help."

"Did you realize at the time that Mr. Snyder was dead?"

"It seemed so. I didn't touch him. I've been through this before, when an elderly gentleman died in his room. The police said don't touch anything."

"That's right. When and how did you find Mr. Snyder?"

"I was cleaning the empty rooms on the eighth floor last night around ten o'clock. I thought I heard a noise, so I stepped into the stairwell to see. We've had a problem with mice lately, and I thought, oh, no, one of the guests will see a mouse, and we'll have trouble. So I looked and I saw this form on the steps. I went down and looked closer. It was a man all curled up. He looked very dead, and there was a lot of blood, so I ran back to the eighth floor and took the elevator down to the lobby—not screaming—and told the desk clerk. The police came, asked me the same questions you're asking, and took the body away. I learned later it was a Mr. Snyder, a guest of the hotel. A very sad business."

"You didn't see or hear anything else in the stairwell?"

"Nothing," she said. "I don't know how long he was there, or what he was doing on the stairs. Most people take the elevator."

"Who else besides the cleaning service and guests uses the stairs?" I asked.

"Sometimes builders, repairmen, other hotel staff members. These science-fiction people will be all over the place. They like to have pretend battles. They'll chase each other up and down the stairs and down the halls. It's silly, but they're not messy. They don't tear up the rooms."

"Where are they located?"

"The sixth floor has quite a few already. I know because they have on costumes. The rest are scattered."

I thanked her for her help. Could Sean Snyder have gotten

in the way of a science fiction battle? But the people who came to conventions used water guns and plastic light sabers, toy stuff. Certainly not real knives—or did they?

I took the elevator to the ninth floor and tried to get near the crime scene, but no luck. Cops guarded the elevators on the sixth, seventh, and eighth floors, and wouldn't let anyone off who didn't have a room key. I walked around looking for imaginary ice machines, but found out nothing. I returned to the lobby.

Geoff arrived, back from the station, looking worn and tired. We went to the eighth floor, this time getting past the cop in the hall after Geoff flashed his keycard. I followed him into his room.

"Any luck?" he asked me.

"Not yet. Give it to me straight, Geoff. Who had it in for Sean?"

Geoff opened the mini bar, picked up one of the small liquor bottles, drank the contents in one gulp, and set it down. "We ruined lots of careers. That's the whole idea. Those people don't have a right to make a living by conning others."

"Anyone ever threaten him?"

He shook his head. "They usually slink off with their tails between their legs. Sean and I did a lot of good by getting rid of those people. They didn't deserve success."

I ignored the various obvious comebacks to such remarks. "Hate mail? Phone calls in the middle of the night?"

"A few, but no actual face to face confrontations. They knew better than to go up against us. We had the truth on our side." He started to drink another bottle, decided against it, and put it down with a clank.

"Did you ever take down anyone associated with the science fiction or fantasy community? Any problem with gamers? Comic book fans?"

"We've dealt with all kinds. They're all insane."

"It would help if you could think of someone in particular."

With an angry gesture, he swept the table clear. The little bottles bounced on the carpet. "No one has ever been able to prove their so-called talent! Do you understand what I'm saying to you? No one ever said, 'Here, let me show you how I can levitate.' 'Let

me tell you exactly what you're thinking.' Because they couldn't.
They were all frauds...except..." His anger drained away. "Except
Camden knew this was going to happen, and in spite of every-
thing, he tried to warn Sean. I have trouble believing that."

"That he saw Sean's murder, or that he tried to warn you?"

"Both."

There was a knock on the door. Geoff let Camden in.

"Did you find anything?"

Camden sat down on the bed. He looked a couple of shades
paler than usual. "Whoever killed Sean hated him a great deal."

Geoff looked puzzled. "Hated him? Who was it? Did you see
the murderer?"

I went to the bathroom, unwrapped one of the plastic cups,
filled it with water, and brought it back to Camden. He drank slowly and then rubbed his eyes.

"The hatred is so intense it's like standing in front of a blast
furnace. I couldn't see any features. But it was personal. It had to
be someone he knew."

Geoff's voice shook with emotion, his eyes pleading. "But not
me, right? You couldn't have seen or felt me!"

"No, Geoff," Camden said. "I know you didn't kill Sean, and I
sensed nothing at the scene that indicated you were there."

"Did you tell the police? Will they listen to you?"

"Jordan will, but he'll have a hard time explaining why to his
colleagues."

"What about Sean's room? Did they let you look in there?"

"Yes, but I didn't sense anything."

"Geoff," I said. "What were you and Sean planning to do at
ExtravaganzaCon?"

"We were supposed to have a presentation on how people are
fooled into believing in UFOs. And we have a table in the dealers'
room for our books. What's that got to do with anything?"

"It's possible someone has come to the convention to settle
a score with you and your brother for challenging their theories
about the unknown."

He took a breath and his voice steadied. "Recently, Sean and
I disproved several UFO sightings, so those people are not happy

with us. But they're west coast, so I don't think they're here. We also had a run in with a fellow who sells crystals and claims they have healing powers. His name is Bob Plank. Sean and I proved his claims were false, and he sent quite a few nasty emails. He's also one of those idiots who believe the moon landing was staged. We took him to task about that, as well. He might be here."

"I know this is going to be hard," I said, "but I want you to attend the convention with us tomorrow. If you're up to it."

Geoff's eyes filled with tears. "It won't be hard. Finding out who killed my brother is all that will keep me going."

CHAPTER SIX

"Fire Maidens From Outer Space"

Camden and I got back to the house around two-thirty AM. We managed to stagger up around nine, which meant revising our convention plans. To make my morning complete, I had a call from Pastor Gary. He was, as usual, pissed.

"I expected an update before now."

"Even the Lord took seven days to get the job done," I said. "I'm following the lead you gave me, but it's going to take more than half a day to find the person responsible for those videos." I didn't tell him that I thought a murder case took precedent.

The man's voice quivered with rage. "Those videos will cause irreparable damage to the church! I will not be made a laughing-stock for unbelievers!"

It was a little too late for that. "Excuse me, but hasn't the church weathered all sorts of difficulties over the ages? Are you saying it's not strong enough to overcome this?"

He sputtered for an answer. "Of course the church will overcome! But I want this fraudulent Angel of Truth found and punished and made an example for anyone else who thinks he's above the Word of God. I expect you to call me every day with a report." He hung up.

I checked my ear for scorch marks. What an arrogant old bastard. He wasn't concerned about the church. He was concerned about his own image. A report every day, huh? I would have to see how creative I could be.

Camden agreed with me that solving Sean's murder was much more important than exposing the creator of some ridiculous YouTube videos. So it was better-late-than-never nine-thirty by the time Camden and I headed out to the Parkland Hilton's convention center to gaze upon the glory that is the main room of a full-on multi-genre convention: rows and rows of tables filled with fanzines and comics and games and tee shirts and every possible kind of fan dressed in costume.

I'd opted for a regular shirt, sweat shirt, and khaki slacks. Camden was in his usual disarray: faded jeans, worn sneakers, blue tee shirt, dark blue vest, and blue hoodie. The vest, in honor of the occasion, had yellow stars and planets. We looked amazingly normal. For any other local.

There were lizard men, lizard women, lizard children, and lizard dogs. There were Klingons and Borg and Highlanders. There were lots of things I didn't recognize. And of course, there were large happy fans, their straining tee shirts festooned with buttons, pins, and ribbons. Stuart had come as the jolliest-looking Klingon I'd ever seen. He joined another group of Klingons, who greeted him with chest bumps and battle cries that sounded like they were attempting to cough up steel wool.

Camden and I had decided on a course of action. We'd check out the dealers' room first and look for Bob Plank the crystal seller and then catch the pilot episode of *Doorway to Mars*. Camden wanted to see the UFO exhibits. I wanted to have my picture made with Lucinda Love. We wanted to check out *Vampire Rage*, and definitely check out Clearly Rae, a world-famous filk singer and actress, best known for her role as slightly clad Hris on *River of Stars*. As the news of the murder spread, as it surely would, we'd probe convention attendees and dealers about the Snyders. There was no group on the planet who knew more details about their community than the true fans. Then there might be time to catch another video before Camden had to go home and change clothes for Tea with Mother and Her Friends.

Dealer room first. As we wandered the aisles admiring all the stuff, we kept an eye out for crystals. A few had crystal pendants, earrings, and bracelets, but no one had chunks of crystal.

"Ask down at the end," someone suggested in response to my query.

It took a while to reach the end where we found two empty tables and a small sign that read: "Bob Plank: Shining Examples."

"Know anything about this?" I asked the young woman at the adjoining table. She was dressed as Princess Leia complete with the cinnamon bun hairdo. She was, not surprisingly, selling *Star Wars* memorabilia. Her table was also filled with Ghostbusters tee shirts and toys.

"He's not here yet," she said.

I could see that. "Does he sell crystals?"

"Yeah. I heard he missed his flight or something."

Missed his flight, or took a side trip to the stairwell to encounter Sean Snyder? It was something to consider.

Princess Leia was not interested in crystals or UFOs or psychics. Neither were any of the other dealers we spoke with. I found one fellow dressed as Neo from *The Matrix* who, when prompted, admitted he had read the Snyders' *Take Charge of Your Own Destiny*, which he said had some cool ideas, but he didn't know anything about the authors. It was clear that word of Sean's murder had not reached this end of the room yet.

"It was an okay book, but it didn't make me want to read any of their others," he said.

I thought I'd hit pay dirt when I asked a group of teens in *Mad Max* costumes if they'd ever heard of anyone who debunked UFO sightings, and one remarked that people like that were scum. But it turned out the group was calling everyone and everything scum to keep in character. Camden and I moved on.

We had a SF-packed morning, ate a couple of space burgers, drank some Tang, and were on our way to the Magnolia Room to hear filk-singer Clearly Rae when we passed a group of Japanese anime fans who stared at Camden and got all excited.

"Wow, mister, you could be Quatre Winner on *Gundam Wing*. Doesn't he look like Quatre, guys?"

They gathered around, delighted. "If they ever do a live-action version, you oughta be in it," one man said.

"Wow, even the hair's the same. How did you get it to do that?"

"Did you mean to come as Quatre?"

"This is really something!"

It took a while to disengage Camden from his new fans and move along. "It's always a treat to be among your people," I said.

"It's great," he said. "I enjoy being compared to a cartoon character."

"Quatre's the wimp, isn't he?"

"The sensitive one."

"Wimp."

"He can pilot one of those monster suits and shoot the crap out of his enemies."

"Yeah, but he feels bad about it later."

Camden started to tell me something uncomplimentary when he stopped in the aisle. "Randall. Look. The Enforcettes."

Striding toward us came three tall, amazingly fit young women in tiny, cleavage-and-thigh-enhancing fantasy outfits. They halted and introduced themselves as Tiger, Brianna, and Dawn. Camden and I already knew this. *Enforcettes 3000* was one of our guilty pleasures, a wacky syndicated SF show about three warrior women in a future world called Atlantia. The gals kept themselves in leather and chrome by hiring out as mercenaries and bodyguards, always saving the last ten minutes of the show for a series of karate acrobatics and explosions. Good senseless fun, and always a chance someone might pop out of the gravity-defying costumes.

These young women had done their homework. They looked exactly like the characters. Tiger was a sleek black woman with incredible abs, huge dark eyes made up Egyptian style, and her long hair in a complicated series of braided loops. Brianna had spiky red hair and an expression that said, "Just try it." She was also tall, elegantly muscled, and generously tattooed. Dawn had blank blue eyes, blonde hair cut in rough bangs, and long lean legs that could've easily straddled me and Camden at the same time.

"We're the Enforcettes," Tiger said, "and we want you to help us with our cosplay presentation. You're perfect."

As I tried to think of a modest reply, I realized all three women were looking at Camden, or rather, looking down at Camden, since all three were at least my height of six feet.

"Perfect?" he said.

I was surprised his voice was steady. Surrounding us, with all that skin on display, the Enforcettes were putting forth considerable heat.

"Yes," Tiger said. "For the cosplay contest tonight at seven, we want to dramatize the rescue of the Star Prince, episode forty-four, *The Crown of Rutan*. The fellow who was supposed to take part backed out at the last minute, but you're a much better choice. All you have to do is lie on the floor and let me pick you up." She smiled, showing beautiful teeth. A skull had been carved into one incisor. "I promise I'll be gentle."

"Well, I, um," Camden said as all three leaned in.

"You've seen the show?" Brianna asked.

He nodded.

"Then you know we always get our way. How about it, sport? Meet us in Ballroom A at five-thirty."

Dawn reached out and ran her hand through his hair. "Nice," she said.

The Enforcettes strode off, people parting quickly to let them by.

"Impressive," someone in the crowd said.

I watched the graceful swing of three very attractive rear ends. "I've got another word for it."

Camden was standing still, taking deep breaths.

"Going to do it?" I asked. "It's a dream come true. Carried off by the Enforcettes."

"I'm trying to remember what happened in that episode."

"I'd say the Star Prince got really lucky."

"Now I definitely hate to leave."

"I'll keep the girls company till you get back."

Camden and I wandered into the Magnolia Room, where Clearly Rae was singing. Clearly Rae was a beautiful woman, but filk-singing is an acquired taste, the science fiction equivalent of folk singing. Fans change the words to fit their favorite shows. We stood at the back and listened for a while. Then we decided to move on.

"There's just too much," Camden said. "We need at least two weeks."

My cell phone rang. It was Geoff Snyder. "Are you at the convention?" he asked. "Yes," I said. "Where can I meet you?"

"I need some time," he said. "I've been at the police station all morning. I just got back. Give me an hour and I'll meet you at the north elevators."

Stuart and his Klingon buddies came up, hawking and gacking. Stuart's headpiece made him look like a Bigfoot truck had run across his forehead. "Hey, guys," he said, "did you know there's going to be a demonstration of Pik-Ra fighting in the Azalea Room? Come on, it's down this hall. They're going to do light saber battles, too."

Pik-Ra was a special alien knife fighting used on *Nebula Fortress*. It was kind of cool, but I didn't need to see it live. "No, thanks. We're going to catch some of *Diamond Hunter*."

"This is a great con, isn't it? See you later."

Diamond Hunter was a lot clunkier than either Camden or I remembered. Halfway through the pilot episode, I said, "Let's get another drink," and Camden didn't argue. He had another Coke and then it was time for Jean Belton's tea. I had to meet Geoff Snyder, so I made sure Camden got a taxi to take him to the country club.

Geoff was standing at the north elevators. He looked exhausted but determined. "What am I supposed to do?" he said.

"Bob Plank has a table in the dealers' room, but he isn't here yet," I said. "Let's take a walk around and see if any of your nemeses are here."

"I don't see why anyone is here." He gave a disgusted glance at the costumed fans. "I can't believe grown people do this. My interest is real life, not all this fantasy nonsense." He paused. "Oh, God. I need to take care of this."

"This" was a table filled with the Snyders' books. A few people were looking through the stacks, reading the back covers, and thumbing through the brochures.

"Sean and I were going to sell and sign books before and after our presentation," Geoff said. His voice was dull. "No way I can do that now."

I knew huge conventions like ExtravaganzaCon had armies of volunteers. "We'll get someone to pack them up for you."

"Yes," he said. He picked up one of the books and turned it to the picture of himself and Sean on the back. He set it down without another word.

We wandered around the exhibits and dealers' tables, Geoff making snide remarks about living in fantasy worlds. I tried not to comment—I mean, the guy had just lost his brother—but Geoff was one sorry whiner. I had the feeling he was that way in or out of mourning. Nothing quite like a frustrated ballet dancer.

We viewed everyone in the main hall, but Geoff didn't recognize anyone he knew. "These people are jokes," he said. "Isn't there anybody doing serious work?"

"There's an art show."

"Let's go there."

He was aghast at some of the sexually explicit drawings in the art room, but found a few abstracts he liked and a few realistic paintings of planets he grudgingly admired.

"But this is horrible."

We'd paused in front of a large canvas depicting death and destruction. Body parts littered a floor smeared with bright red blood, and alien flies with huge wings and nasty-looking mouths danced around the corpses. Even the edges of the canvas had been cut rough and jagged so it looked chewed. "I have to agree with you on this one." I said.

"What sort of sick mind thinks up such images?"

"It's not sick," a young woman dressed like someone out of Sherwood Forest said. "It's a scene from *Chaos Planet*, second season. The painting is called *Gallery of Fear.*"

"Is this your work?" I didn't want to insult the artist.

"Mine? I can only dream of being this good. It's an original Leena Fay." She pointed to the info sheet displayed beside *Gallery of Fear.*

"Does she think someone will actually buy this monstrosity?" Geoff asked.

The young woman pointed to a card hanging under the painting. "NFS. Not For Sale. It's from her private collection."

"It should've stayed there."

Geoff moved away to the next set of paintings. The young woman made a face at his back. "I suppose he knows everything there is to know about art."

"He's a little grumpy today," I said.

"I love Leena Fay's work. There's something so profound about it. You can almost believe she lived it."

"Body parts and giant flies? No, thanks."

"I mean the turmoil, the agony. Her sister died horribly, and she's never gotten over it. There are rumors. . ."

"When was this?"

"A couple of years ago. That's when her work took this dark turn."

"Is Leena Fay here, at this convention?"

"She's in the program, so she'd better be." The young woman took a copy of the convention book from a nearby display table and turned to a page near the back. "See? She's doing a panel Monday on 'The Effect of Emotion on Artistic Creations.'"

Camden and I hadn't paid much attention to the art section of the book. The photo of the artist showed a dark-haired woman with a melancholy expression and a look in her blue eyes that could only be described as haunted. She was elegantly dressed in a gray suit and pink blouse. Her only jewelry was a silver pin shaped like an "M" on the suit jacket lapel.

"What's the 'M' for?" I asked the young woman. Morose? Mirthless? Morbid?

"I'm not sure," she said. "Maybe it's part of her mystique."

"Thank you." I took another look at Leena Fay's picture. Could she be the sad lady Lindsey wanted me to help?

I joined Geoff at the sculptures. He was shaking his head at the sight of lopsided dragons, phallic spaceships, and lumpy jewelry.

"This is hopeless," he said.

I didn't know if he meant the artwork or our search. "Camden should be back soon. Maybe he can help out."

He took another look around the art room. "Sean and I never understood the attraction of these conventions. As far as we were concerned, science fiction was for people who couldn't deal with reality, the same people who run to psychics and Ouija Boards to solve their problems." A group of people dressed as Reticulated Grays walked by, waving their long fingers. Geoff gave me a disgusted look. "I'm really very tired. I'm going back to my room. I'll talk to you later."

CHAPTER SEVEN

"The Angry Red Planet"

I stopped by the desk at the art room door and inquired about Leena Fay's sister. The man in charge was dressed as a wizard, purple robe with gold stars and a large floppy purple hat. He was rearranging small metallic prints of wizards and dragons on a screen of silver mesh, but paused to answer my question.

"A tragic death, but no, not a murder. We're all pleased to see Leena's working again, though her style is radically different."

"Her work wasn't always this strong?"

He readjusted his hat. "Oh, my, no. Fairies and moonbeams before, the lightest most delicate stuff you can imagine. Nothing like the paintings she does now."

I wandered back to the dealers' room, but the "Shining Examples" tables were still empty.

Camden got back at four-thirty. His hair was still combed, and he hadn't bothered to change back into his convention wear, so he looked extremely neat in his dark gray suit and burgundy tie. He was carrying his copy of the first *Dark Star* book.

"How'd it go?" I asked.

"Pretty good, actually. I got two weddings and another evening concert out of it."

"There's a gross painting I want you to see."

"Can it wait? I have just enough time to get my book signed."

"Hey, guys!"

"Here's our favorite Klingon," I said.

Stuart came up as we joined the line to meet Iris Hudson, author of the *Dark Star* series. He had a large canvas tote bag with the con logo on it. He began digging in the bag, hauling out things for us to see. "I got my Batman Super Spectacular signed by the artist, I've got a tee shirt from Lucinda Love, I've got my own personalized Pik-Ra battle knife for when me and the other Klingons have our own convention, I've got the latest *Space Ranger* calendar. Oh, and look! A genuine rock used on the set of *Two For the Stars*. Can you believe it? It only cost me ten dollars."

I'd never seen a picture of Iris Hudson, but from her books, I'd decided she was a rangy athletic brunette with an amusingly sarcastic outlook on life, not unlike my own. Don't ever judge an author by her covers. I got only one thing right: she was brunette. She was also heavyset, scowling, and condescending. Every request for an autograph brought a sigh and a quick disinterested scribble.

Camden looked daunted. "She doesn't seem to be enjoying this, does she?"

"It's hard for royalty to go out among the peasants."

The woman in line in front of Camden was oblivious to Hudson's bored contempt. She plunked down a shiny copy of *Danger Star*.

"Ms. Hudson, I absolutely love the *Dark Star* series. When Kaspar Wildhaven carried Elphinia Day Star off to his spaceship, I just got cold chills. You really are a remarkable writer."

Hudson ignored the compliment. "How do you want this signed?"

"To Terri—that's with an 'I.'"

"Of course it is." Iris Hudson scrawled illegibly on the inside cover and shoved the book forward. She turned to the tall dark-haired man beside her, who was reading something on his cell phone. He had a long serious face and a hawk like nose, and like Hudson, appeared to be in his fifties. "Parnell, how much longer do I have to sit here?"

He glanced at his phone. "Fifteen minutes."

"Close enough." She heaved herself out of her chair. Camden was next in line. Two more people stood behind him, a man dressed as the Green Hornet in a trench coat, fedora, and black mask, and a woman in flowing purple robes and antenna. Hudson gave Camden a brief glance. "Sorry, shorty."

"Hey," I said. "What's a few more people? It won't take five minutes."

She ignored me, gathering up a large pocketbook and a bottle of water.

"These people are the reason you're famous. Show a little consideration."

She glared. "I've been sitting here for two effing hours, listening to these people gush and jabber, when they haven't the slightest comprehension of the real meaning of my work. It's insulting."

"Are you talking about the underlying existentialism?" Camden asked.

"Or the relationship of the Dark System to chaos theory?" the Green Hornet said.

"Or the feminist principles that guide the Charter of Unified Planets?" Antenna Woman said.

Any other author would have been flattered and impressed. Not Mrs. Ego-Head. "There's a lot more to it than that." She turned to go.

"Aw, come on!" the man dressed as the Green Hornet said. "It's not five yet."

She offered no apology. She turned her back and walked away. The serious man went with her. I started after them to say something appropriate, but Camden caught my arm.

"It's not worth it."

"Let him punch her out," the Green Hornet said. "I'd consider that worth a lot. Who does she think she is? They shouldn't have authors come who don't want to meet their fans."

"Maybe she's just having a bad day," Camden said.

"No, she's first class bitch. I'm telling the con organizers." He strode off.

"Gosh," Stuart said.

Antenna Woman put her book back into a multicolored bag decorated with fairies and unicorns. She had short graying hair and a pleasant face. Maybe a little older than your typical fairy, but this was ExtravaganzaCon, a definite no-judgment zone. "Iris Hudson has a reputation for being rude. At PixieCon last August she got in a fight on the elevator with some folks who questioned her use of tense in *Dark Territories*. It was a harmless question, but she flew into a rage. And then there's the Dark Feud with the Faerie community."

Not just a feud, but a Dark Feud. "Any idea what makes her so touchy?" I asked.

"Oh, I've known her awhile, and she's always been a bit ornery."

"So she wouldn't even sign a book for a fairy friend?"

"Once the *Dark Star* series became famous, she left her fairy friends in the pixie dust," Antenna Woman said. "I thought she might be a little glad to see me. Guess I was wrong." She checked her heavily jeweled watch. "Well, I've got just enough time to get to the panel on Fantasy World Building. I will see you gentlemen around, I'm sure." She hurried off in a swirl of purple.

I turned to Camden. "I'd like Iris Hudson to be the murderer. Maybe Sean and Geoff gave one of her books a bad review."

Camden looked down at the beautiful cover of *Dark Star* as if he couldn't quite understand how such an angry woman could write such poetry. I picked up one of the black markers Hudson had left on the table. "Here, I'll sign your book. You won't be able to tell the difference."

He looked up and over in Hudson's direction, his expression thoughtful. Then he touched the table where she'd leaned her elbows.

"I hope you're seeing something painful and disgusting in her future."

He shook his head. "It's not good."

"The way she treats people, I'm not surprised."

"I think I'd better talk to her."

"And get your head taken off? Is it that serious?"

"I can't tell. I'm getting a lot of negative energy."

"From that pleasant young flower? I'm shocked." I took out my phone. "I'll ask Geoff if he knows her."

Geoff answered on the first ring. "Any news?"

"Did you or Sean ever antagonize a large surly science fiction author named Iris Hudson?" I asked. "She's written a series of *Dark Star* books."

He made an exasperated sound. "Neither Sean nor I ever read science fiction. The name doesn't ring a bell, Randall. Has Plank shown up yet? What has he got to say?"

"He still isn't here."

"Let me know the minute he arrives. I want a word with him."

Geoff ended the call. I put my phone away. "It's almost five," I said to Camden. "We need to get to Ballroom A and see what the Enforcettes have planned. Stuart, you with us?"

He shook his head. "I'd love to meet the Enforcettes, but I've got the Klingon initiation ceremony at five."

"That sounds like a fun-filled Klingon activity."

Stuart and Irony have not been properly introduced. He beamed. "It sure does!"

***

In Ballroom A, the Enforcettes were trying out karate moves on each other. I watched in admiration as Tiger flipped Dawn over her shoulder and then cart wheeled over to us. She wasn't even breathing hard.

"You didn't have to dress up," she said to Camden, "but I like it. We didn't get your names."

Now she was including me. "I'm David Randall, and this is Camden."

"Welcome to the show, David. Camden, you won't mind if we take off this jacket?" She had it off of him before either of us could blink. She smiled down at him lazily. "And we'll just loosen this tie, okay?"

His expression plainly said, what have I gotten myself into? "Okay."

"Good. Now, lie face down over there and close your eyes. Do you remember episode forty-four? The evil prime minister has betrayed the prince and left him to the Morgs, so you've been in the

Morg dungeon for a couple of days. We've got a couple of guys to be Morgs, and we're going to beat the snot out of them. All you have to do is stay over there out of the way."

"Anything I can do?" I asked.

Brianna looked me up and down. "I've got something you can do later—much later, if you're interested."

"If we were doing episode eighty, you'd make a perfect Count Leo," Dawn said, "but there's not much fighting in that one."

Tiger sauntered up and gave me a skull-shiny smile. "You're way too handsome to be a Morg. How about if you watch and give us some pointers?"

I pulled up a chair. Two large men dressed in leather and chains came growling in. The girls, screaming shrill battle cries, attacked. The fight was well-choreographed, with plenty of yells and smacks. It didn't take long for the Enforcettes to dispatch the Morgs, but then two more lumbered in.

Brianna yelled, "Get the prince! We'll take care of these two!"

Tiger ran and scooped up Camden. She carried him to the far end of the ballroom, and then cart wheeled back to the fray. As soon as the remaining Morgs were defeated, all three women went to Camden.

"We need a good finish," Dawn said.

"All right," Tiger said, "we know the Star Prince is grateful for the rescue." She gave him a long stare and smiled. "Very grateful."

"PG-13 grateful," Brianna said. "At this con, anyway."

"How about if we come out and strike some poses?" She turned to me. "What do you think?"

The four big guys who played the Morgs came up, readjusting their armor and rubbing their elbows and knees.

"The fight is your best part," I said. "The Morgs can stagger up afterwards and go off in the other direction."

Tiger and the Morgs nodded. "I like it. It shows we won, and people can decide for themselves what happened next. Any other suggestions?"

"At the beginning, why don't you have two of the Morgs carry Camden in and dump him? They can kick him and growl and carry on. Make it more threatening."

"Thanks a lot," Camden said.

"You can take your time on that first fight. Make it look as if you might not win. How long do you have for your skit?"

"No more than five minutes."

I picked out the two biggest Morgs. "At the start, you guys drag Camden in, slap him around, have a good laugh. Then when the girls come in, act like it's no big deal to fight them. Tiger, let them get the upper hand for a while, and then you can start wiping the floor with them."

"Great," she said. "Let's try it."

Camden took off his shoes. The Morgs dragged him in, tossed him down, and gave him a couple of fake kicks. Then they dusted their hands and whacked each other on the back. When Tiger and Brianna arrived, the guys continued to laugh until Tiger's foot connected with a Morg belly and the fight was on. This time, it was much more convincing to have the Enforcettes come from behind to win the battle. When it was all over, everyone agreed the performance was better.

Dawn gave Camden a kiss. "You really look unconscious."

"I've had lots of practice," he said.

The Morgs said they'd see us at the contest and left to repair their costumes. Tiger beamed at me. "Thanks very much, David. You guys want to get a bite with us before the show?"

"I'd be happy to," I said. It was after six and I was ready to eat. "But I should tell you Camden's married, and I'm in a very good relationship."

"Aww," Dawn said.

"I don't think Ellie would mind if we bought the Enforcettes a soda," Camden said.

"Especially if we don't tell her."

"Maybe some pizza at the Flying Saucer?"

Dawn took his arm. "I never met a pizza I didn't like."

Since the Flying Saucer was in the food court set up for the convention right in the middle of everything, I couldn't see how Ellin would object. It was certainly entertaining to be sitting with the three hottest women at the con, although I gently discouraged Brianna's foot from exploring my leg.

I told the Enforcettes I was working on a murder case, which impressed the hell out of them. I asked them if they knew Geoff and Sean Snyder. They shook their heads. "Are they fans of the show?" Dawn asked.

I couldn't imagine the Snyders watching anything remotely like "The Enforcettes." "Maybe. They made their living debunking psychics and conspiracy believers. Till Sean was murdered. Here at the hotel. Last night."

"Oh, wow." Brianna took another slice of pizza. "Do you have any suspects?"

"I just started my investigation."

Dawn shuddered. "It's kinda creepy, isn't it? Maybe the murderer is walking around the con."

"It would be easy to hide in here," I said. "Better be on the lookout."

Brianna gave me another intense look. "Don't worry. We can protect you."

"I'm counting on it."

Tiger looked at Brianna. "Should we tell them?"

"Guess we'd better."

Camden and I looked puzzled. Dawn made a face. "Oh, him," she said. "Yeah, tell them, Tiger."

"Speaking of being on the lookout," Tiger said, "there's a man who always tries to spoil our skits."

"Eric O'Conner," Brianna said. "My ex."

What? "Whoa, hold on," I said. "Eric O'Connor's your ex-husband?"

"Yes. He's an annoying, obnoxious pest. He'll probably show up tonight right in the middle of our presentation. It's his idea of fun. So if you see someone getting ready to run across the stage or throw something, you have our permission to knock his head off."

"Eric O'Connor who was recently fired from a job at Freedom Path United Church?"

"Maybe. I heard something about some church job, which is crazy, because what's he doing working at a church?"

This sounded too good to be true. "All right, let me make sure I have this straight. I've been trying to get in touch with a man named Eric O'Connor in regard to some unflattering videos of the pastor posted by someone calling himself the Angel of Truth. Does this sound like something your ex-husband would do?"

"Angel of Truth sounds exactly like something he'd make up. He thinks he's God's gift to the world of role playing. I'm not surprised you can't reach him. He's probably down in his bat cave."

"Do you have any idea why he'd go after a pastor like that?"

"I don't have any idea why he does anything."

Dawn brightened. "Maybe he's the murderer! You could arrest him. Then he'd be out of our hair."

"What does he look like?" I asked.

The Enforcettes shared a disgusted look.

"He'll be in some kind of costume," Brianna said. "He's always in costume. He's about your height, but he's scrawny with brown hair and brown eyes. His nose is kinda crooked from where I broke it."

"What kind of costume does he wear?"

"That's the problem. He could be somebody different every day. One day he might be Batman, one day the Green Hornet—"

"There was a man dressed like the Green Hornet standing in the signing line behind Camden. He got riled when Hudson didn't sign his book and stormed off to tell the con organizers."

"That's Eric," Brianna said. "Always the victim."

"Okay, then, I've got some idea of what he looks like. I'll do my best."

"What time is it?" Dawn asked.

As the Enforcettes' abbreviated costumes didn't allow watches, I checked my watch. "Quarter to seven."

"Good. I want to practice a few moves. Come on, girls."

The Enforcettes left to practice. "Can you believe this?" I said to Camden. "If it's the same guy, then I can solve two problems at once, the identity of the Angel of Truth and whoever murdered Sean Snyder."

But I had to find him first.

CHAPTER EIGHT

"Killers From Space"

The cosplay contest was the first big event of the con, which meant it went on forever. First was the contest for the younger contestants with categories that included Most Original, Best Use of Duck Tape, and Scariest Monster. Around eight thirty, the adult contest began with single participants, followed by groups. We stood backstage with the Enforcettes, who enjoyed critiquing the competition and admiring some of the fantastical costumes. At long last, around nine-thirty, it was time for the Star Prince to be rescued. The Enforcettes' skit was a rousing success and took first prize in the group division, a large gold trophy that looked like a shooting star. No one tried to crash the skit or throw anything. I didn't really expect them to. Not that I didn't believe the women, but it seemed far-fetched that anyone would care enough to disrupt the show.

The awards ceremony ended at ten o'clock. As we were going to celebrate with a crowd of admiring fans before heading home, a man dressed as the Green Hornet suddenly pushed through the crowd and snatched the trophy out of Brianna's hands. Camden grabbed his arm to stop him, but the man flung him off and onto the floor and then ran across the convention hall. Brianna set off in hot pursuit, shrieking like a banshee. For a moment, I thought this was another part of the skit the girls had rehearsed earlier, but when Tiger and Dawn swore in anger and tore after the culprit, fantasy and reality began to shift. People scattered in all directions, some helping the chase, some hindering by getting in the way.

"Over here! Over here!" someone dressed as a robot called.

I hauled Camden to his feet and we joined the chase. I caught a glimpse of Brianna's bright red hair as she vaulted over a row of chairs. Someone's light saber blinded me for a moment, and then I saw Dawn shoving people out of her way, pummeling them furiously. The crowd bunched and parted. As Camden and I attempted to swim upstream, I heard Tiger shout:

"You'll pay for this, you coward!"

We reached the front doors of the convention hall. Part of the crowd ran out in a noisy pack, yelling and laughing. Other people kept getting in my way. I couldn't see Camden or any of the Enforcettes. Out of nowhere, Brianna caught my arm.

"I knew things went too smoothly," she said. "It was O'Conner. He waited until after the contest to make his move, the jerk. He got away with our trophy! And look at this!" She held up a piece of sleeve. "It's ruined!"

Since she wasn't wearing very much to begin with, I wasn't sure where to look. Tiger and Camden ran up to us. Camden's tie was askew and his shirt tail was out, but this wasn't an unusual look for him. Tiger's costume was still on, but her impressive bosom heaved with indignation.

"I cannot believe he had the nerve to do that! Where is he?"

"Dawn chased him out," Brianna said. "I know she can catch him."

But Dawn jogged back in from the parking lot empty handed.

"You let him get away?" Tiger said. "Dawn! This was the perfect opportunity to snag the bastard."

"I'm sorry!" she said. "I almost had him, and a van pulled out between us. When I could get around, he'd disappeared."

"What about our trophy?" Brianna asked.

"I guess he's still got it."

Tiger turned to me. "You see what a problem he is. He'd better not come back."

Brianna ground her fist in her palm. "If he does, we'll be ready for him."

All around us, people laughed and commented on the action. Everyone else at the cosplay contest seemed to think O'Conner's stunt was part of the show. I couldn't figure out why he felt the need to be such a distraction. Maybe he was a frustrated actor in addition to being a serial troublemaker. Or maybe he had another motive for causing all the commotion.

The Enforcettes were too tough to cry, but they sure looked like they wanted to.

"Let's see if he ditched the trophy somewhere," I said.

We walked all around the outside of the convention center and the hotel. Near the back we found a row of Dumpsters. As I boosted Camden up for a look inside, Brianna said, "You don't have to do that."

"Are you kidding?" I said. "Camden used to live in these things."

"Not exactly," he said. "But I have been known to sleep in one."

We checked all the Dumpsters and trash cans and looked in the shrubs and flower beds. Then we took a walk through the parking lot, but we didn't find the trophy. As we circled around to the front door, several police cars rolled up, lights flashing, followed by an ambulance.

"Good," Tiger said. "I'm glad someone called the cops."

Jordan Finley, large, square, and annoyed, grimaced when he saw me. "I'm not surprised to see you two here."

"What's going on?" I asked.

"Someone's found a body."

"I hope it's Eric O'Conner," Brianna said.

Jordan raised an eyebrow.

"Meet the Enforcettes," I said. "Tiger, Brianna, and Dawn."

"I know who the Enforcettes are, Randall."

"We were taking part in a cosplay contest," Tiger said. "Cam and David were with us. What's this all about?"

Jordan's grim expression told me this was not the time to answer questions. "We'll talk tomorrow," I told the Enforcettes. "And we'll find your trophy."

Tiger tugged on Dawn's arm. "We need to go."

After the Enforcettes left, Camden said, "It's Iris Hudson, isn't it?"

Now both Jordan's eyebrows went all the way up into his hairline.

"I saw something earlier today, but there was so much negative energy, I couldn't tell what was going to happen. I didn't have a chance to warn her."

I wasn't going to let Camden blame himself for whatever happened to Iris Hudson. "You saw what kind of mood she was in. She wouldn't have listened to you or to anyone." I turned to Jordan. "You may have trouble on this one. Iris Hudson was extremely rude to her fans. She even turned Camden down, and he was wearing his suit. From the way people talked about her, she had plenty of enemies."

Jordan held a brief conversation with someone who must have been at the crime scene. "I'll be up in a minute," he told them. He gave Camden a keen glance. "The victim is indeed Iris Hudson. When did you two last see her?"

"Just before five," I said. "I was waiting for Camden to get his book signed. She acted real snotty, refused to sign the last few books, packed up and left. The guy behind Camden was the same man who caused a big commotion in the convention and ran out the door. Eric O'Conner."

"Description?"

"About my height, brown hair, brown eyes. He was wearing a Green Hornet costume. The Enforcettes won the costume contest, and he stole their trophy."

"Any idea why he'd do that?"

"Brianna's his ex-wife. He has issues"

Jordan wrote this down. "Did O'Conner have issues with Iris Hudson?"

"He was pretty angry when she didn't sign his book."

His sharp little blue eyes dared me to withhold information. "Anything else?"

"The other person in line with Camden was a woman with antennae. I didn't get her name."

"So Hudson ignores the last people in line and, as far as you know, goes to her room around five."

"Right."

His phone buzzed, and he spoke with another member of his team for several minutes before ending the call. He turned to us. "Go home."

"Are you shutting down the con?"

"For tonight, yes. If we finish what needs to be done, the con can open tomorrow—maybe."

"Can you give me some details?"

"I'd be a lot happier if you'd stop causing murders, Randall." He started to say something else, probably "Back off," when the hotel's front doors slid open, and a woman in a white blouse and gray suit woman in a suit approached him. She had dark hair and dark eyes and the serious look of person in charge with grim news to report.

She introduced herself to Jordan as the head of hotel security. "Here's what we know so far, Detective Finley. Iris Hudson was found dead in her room. She was stabbed—the knife was still in the wound. Her manager was the last one to see her. He said she went up to her room around five to take a nap. He wasn't to disturb her until eight, when she had a round table conference with some other authors. He knocked on her door a few minutes before eight. She answered and told him she didn't want to go to the conference. When he came back at ten, she didn't answer the door or his phone call. He got concerned, had security open the door, and we found her." She checked her notes on her phone. "The murder weapon had a name on it. Stuart King."

Camden and I rocked back.

No way! "Stuart?" I said. "Stuart King?" This had to be some ridiculous mistake. Then I thought of Stuart's purchases. "You don't mean a Pik-Ra knife?"

She gave me a look as if to say, "And what is your business here?" "If a Pik-Ra knife has a curved edge with uneven teeth and 'Stuart King' on the handle, then yes, that's what I mean."

Stuart's personalized Pik-Ra knife he was so proud of. "I thought all those things were plastic."

"Not this one."

What the hell? "Jordan, you know Stuart isn't a murderer."

"Was he with you tonight?" Jordan asked.

After Iris Hudson abruptly ended her book signing, Stuart had left with his Klingon friends. I didn't remember seeing him or any of the Klingons at the cosplay contest, but then, my attention was on the Enforcettes. "No. Somebody must have stolen the knife from his bag."

"We'll see about that." He thanked the woman for the information and said he'd be right up to the scene of the crime. She gave him a nod and returned to the hotel.

Camden had listened with growing alarm. "Jordan, he didn't do it. I'd know something like that, believe me."

Jordan might be willing to believe Camden, but his fellow officers were not as likely to go with psychic feelings as an alibi. "I've got to do things my way," Jordan said. "Right now, I need to talk to Stuart."

"He isn't under arrest, is he?" Camden asked.

"No, but right now he's obviously a person of interest. If he cooperates with the investigation we may be able to establish an alibi. Just relax. It'll be a casual interview, and if we're satisfied with his story, he can go home."

"I want to see the crime scene."

Jordan's voice was firm. "No."

"What about Parnell, Hudson's manager?" I asked. "Can you corroborate his time line?"

"We're working on it."

Stuart came up to us, followed by another officer. His eyes were round with fear, and his headpiece was crooked. "Guys, did you hear? That woman was killed with my knife, and now the police say they want to talk to me. Do they think I did it? I didn't even know my knife was missing!"

"It's okay," Camden said. "Jordan needs to ask you a few questions."

"Oh, my gosh, this is awful."

"Stuart," I said, "can anybody vouch for your whereabouts?"

"I don't know. I suppose so. I—I really can't think right now."

"Okay. We'll figure it out. Right now, go with this officer and we'll wait for you."

***

We sat down in the hotel lobby to wait. The lobby was eerily quiet, and the beige and brown chairs were plush and comfortable, but neither of us felt like dozing off.

"Well, that was an interesting con experience," I said. "Think this O'Conner character had anything to do with the murder?" He took so long to answer, I thought he'd zoned out. "Camden?"

"I don't know, but he created a hell of a diversion."

"The person who sold Stuart the knife knew it was real. Maybe he hoped it would end up in Hudson. I'll chat with him tomorrow."

Camden glanced toward the hallway where Jordan had taken Stuart. "I hope Stuart will be all right."

"He's cooperating. That says a lot."

"He puts worms back on the lawn."

Camden can be cryptic, but this was obtuse, even by his standards. "Huh?"

"If Stuart sees a worm struggling on the sidewalk, he puts it back in the grass. There's no way he could hurt anyone."

"Iris Hudson wasn't as nice as a worm." I thought back to the signing incident. "You saw something there, but you said it was cloudy."

"That's true. Stuart's involved, and I'm friends with Stuart. I'm too close to what happened. I'm not going to get a clear picture."

He sat with his head in his hands as if willing that picture to clear. I slumped back in my chair, trying to think of how someone could have taken Stuart's knife and why they would stab Iris Hudson. Jordan finished interviewing Stuart around 1 AM. He came wobbling down the hallway. He looked shell-shocked. Camden and I got him to the Fury, and he climbed into the back seat.

"What happened in there?" I asked as I drove home.

"They sure were serious. They must have asked a thousand questions."

Camden turned around in the passenger seat. "You're no longer a suspect, though, are you?"

"I don't think so. I just want to go home. You know I didn't do it."

"Even if I weren't psychic, I'd know you didn't do it."

"When you bought the Pik-Ra knife, didn't you realize it was a real knife and not a plastic copy?" I asked.

"Well, sure," he said. "I would have bought the fake, but the guy said it was the only one he had. It was only twenty-five dollars, plus they put my name on it. The guy did it right there, and it only took a few minutes."

"Yeah, that turned out to be a plus. Who was with you when you bought it?"

"All the rest of the Klingons, about five guys and two girls."

"So they all knew it was real."

"I don't know how many of them were paying attention. There were lots of knives and weapons for sale. Everybody was buying something."

"Give me their names, anyway. I'll check with all of them."

I handed my phone to Camden, and he put the names in my notes.

"When's the last time you saw your knife? You showed it to me and Camden at Iris Hudson's book signing around five, and then you met the rest of the Klingons for an initiation ceremony. How long did that take?"

"About an hour, I guess."

"What did you do after that?"

"After the ceremony we had some hot dogs for our Battle Feast."

"And you feasted for how long?"

"I don't know. Maybe another hour. Then we stopped by the art room to see these cool portraits Shannon had done of Worf, you know, from *Star Trek*, and after that—" he stopped and blushed. "Shannon invited me to her room."

"That's great," Camden said. "She can provide you with an alibi. What time did she ask you to meet her?"

"She said to come on up." Stuart blushed a darker red. "I couldn't find her room. I looked for about thirty minutes, then I ran into that guy from the book signing, and he gave me a look, so I gave up."

"So, it's probably around eight o'clock by then," I said, "and you're wandering around, and I take it that you were on the eighth floor."

"Well, Shannon said her room was on the eighth floor. But I was lost, that's all. I wasn't trying to find Iris Hudson's room. Why would I do that?"

"Did you ever hook up with your Klingonette?"

"I went to the hospitality room and hung around for a while, but I didn't see her. Then I caught the last part of the cosplay competition and all that hoopla about some man stealing a trophy. Was that part of a skit?"

"No. Let's get back to the hospitality room. Who was there? Did you show anybody the knife?"

Stuart thought hard, his features squeezed together. "An Andoran, a couple of lizard men, somebody dressed like the Third Doctor Who, and some other people. I forget. I didn't show anybody the knife. I had some snacks and left."

"Did you put your bag down and leave it for any time?"

Another face squeeze. "Gosh, I don't remember. I may have set it aside when I got my food, but that was only for a couple of seconds."

I'd seen Stuart load his plate at buffet tables. It would have taken more than a couple of seconds. "Stuart, was five o'clock the last time you saw your knife?"

"Oh, I took it out for the initiation ceremony."

"From five to six."

"Yes. Then I put it back in my bag."

"But you don't recall seeing it after that. You didn't take it out in the food court to chop up your hot dogs? Or in the art room?"

"No," he said sadly.

"So sometime after six o'clock, someone took it," I said. "What about when you went to the eighth floor to meet Shannon? Other than Parnell in the hall, did you interact with anyone?"

"No."

"Did you take the elevator? Was there anyone else inside?"

"No one on the way up. On the way down, Vulcans and Borg, mostly. The usual." He looked at me with pleading eyes. "Can you help me, Randall?"

"Of course. But you're cooperating with the police. You didn't know Hudson, so you don't have a motive. I don't think you're going to be charged with anything."

***

We got home around one-thirty AM. Even under his hair, I could see a red mark on Camden's forehead that was going to be a first class bruise. "Is that a star on your forehead?"

He rubbed the mark. "When I grabbed O'Conner's arm, I connected with the trophy."

"So you were really seeing stars."

Stuart made his zombie-like way up the stairs without saying anything else. Ellin was up and tried to hide her coffee cup but she wasn't quite quick enough.

Camden reacted as if he'd found her drinking poison. "Ellie."

"I know. I'm sorry. I couldn't sleep. I only had a little sip. It's not like I'm chugging whiskey."

"You promised you'd stop. You promised you'd take it easy, get more rest, eat better food."

"I will."

"I'm beginning to think you don't want this baby."

"Of course I do. It's just—" she searched for the right word and settled on "—inconvenient. I don't have time to take it easy right now. We're developing some new shows for the network, and I need lots more guests, and I had to argue Reg out of his ridiculous sweepstakes and bake-off and paranormal pageant. Plus, look at me, Cam. I'm only five months and already lumbering around like a barge. Pretty soon I won't be able to do anything. I'll be this fat cow trying to get up out of chairs. Totally useless."

"Being pregnant doesn't mean you have to stop doing everything, does it?"

"Well, maybe I'm not looking forward to being huge and uncomfortable, did you ever think of that? What did you do to your head?" She brushed back his hair and he winced.

"Just a bump."

"Did you collide with a galaxy? The convention must have been pretty wild today. Did you have a good time?"

"Unfortunately, a woman was murdered with Stuart's knife."

"Stuart?" She turned to me. "You have to be joking. What's he doing with a knife?"

"He bought it there," I said.

"Who was murdered?"

"Iris Hudson, author of the *Dark Star* series. Stuart has actually made the world a better place."

Ellin swung her dark blue gaze back to Camden. "Sean Snyder is murdered, Stuart's knife is used to murder someone else, and you take one between the eyes. Somehow a little sip of coffee doesn't compare."

I had to admit she had us there.

CHAPTER NINE

"Unknown World"

I hauled myself out of bed at nine that Sunday morning and went down to the kitchen, where Kary was fixing grits for breakfast. Grits are something I can eat if I'm really hungry. Kary had been asleep when I got home the night before, so I filled her in on Saturday's con events.

"There was a little problem at the convention," I said. "Stuart bought a special kind of fantasy knife and had his name engraved in the handle. Unfortunately, someone stole his knife and used it to stab Iris Hudson to death, and Stuart is a suspect."

She reacted the same way anyone who knew Stuart did. She stopped short. "Stuart? That's crazy. Didn't Cam see who did it?"

I took our bowls to the counter while she brought the butter and cheese. "No, probably because Stuart's a friend."

She sat down and passed me the salt. "David, wasn't Geoff's brother stabbed, too? This isn't the work of another serial killer, is it?"

"That I don't know. But I'm one step closer to finding the Angel of Truth. Eric O'Connor was at the Con."

"The same man you've been trying to reach?"

"Yes. His ex-wife said creating nasty videos would be something he'd do."

"Did she have any idea why he'd do that?"

"When I catch him, that's the first thing I'm going to ask."

"Maybe he enjoys stabbing people, too." She plopped a spoonful of butter into her grits. I'd seen people put milk and sugar on theirs, but we were butter and cheese grits folks at Grace Street.

"Who's Iris Hudson?"

"The author of the *Dark Star* series, a real charmer. She was the kind of woman who made enemies without trying." I got up to refill my coffee cup. "Need some more coffee?"

"No, thanks." Kary slowly stirred her grits. "Has my father happened to say anything about my mother?"

"No. He's too concerned about himself."

"I wonder how she feels about all this."

I sat back down. "Do you want me to find out?"

She took a long time to reply. "I don't think so."

She looked so downcast, I tried my old joke. "Do you want to marry me?"

"Aren't you going to spell it out in grits?"

"Too slippery. Unless you'll let me cheat and use the cheese."

She smiled as she passed the plastic container filled with cheese slices. "Are you sure you want to get married and ruin our relationship?"

The cheese melted in the hot grits before I could form any letters, so I stirred it up. "Missed your chance."

Kary got up to put her bowl in the sink. She hadn't eaten very much. I knew this business with her father was upsetting her more than she was willing to admit. She gave me a kiss. "I'd better go. I'm substituting for the pianist at Emmanuel Baptist. See you at lunch."

Since I didn't get to sit beside her at our church, share a hymnbook, and provide her with tissues, I played hooky from Victory Holiness. Camden was at church, and Ellin and Stuart were still upstairs, so I had the island to myself. I went online and looked for Eric O'Conner's social media. He was definitely a sci-fi and comic book geek. His posts were all about the latest Marvel movies, science fiction TV series, and the continuing *Star Wars* saga. But neither his Facebook or Twitter accounts mentioned Angel of Truth videos. I found this odd, because videos like that would be something to boast about. Parodies of a raving evangelical pastor didn't fit the geek vibe. O'Conner's Instagram account was filled with pictures of Eric in various costumes, including the Green Hornet, Indiana Jones, Batman, Ironman, and someone called Garnon the Great, apparently a superhero O'Conner created. Garnon the Great was all in gold with a snarling face mask and a long staff with a crook at the end. He looked like an annoyed shepherd.

Next, I looked up Iris Hudson. The most recent post informed her followers that Iris had met with an accident during ExtravaganzaCon at the Parkland Hilton in Parkland, NC, and police were still investigating. There were many comments expressing disbelief and sad face emojis. Earlier Facebook and Twitter posts were brief and factual, mainly listing where she would be signing—or not signing—her books.

The Snyders were on Facebook and Twitter, but only to post their scheduled events. Their website had much more information about their books and their goal in life, which was to debunk everything that could be debunked. I'd hoped to find a comment section on the website to get an idea of what people thought of them, but there were no comments, just glowing reviews of their books.

Occasionally I'd hear Ellin dashing to the bathroom to throw up. Around eleven thirty, she came down to the kitchen. She wasn't much of a cook, but like everything else in her life, she always had to prove herself.

I wandered into the kitchen to get a cola. "Are you all right?"

She cracked some eggs and stirred them in a bowl. "Yes, thanks. A little morning sickness."

It was a testament to her toughness that the yellowy mixture wasn't making her heave. "What are you making?"

"Biscuits."

"That sounds good."

She eyed me, looking for signs of sarcasm. I kept my innocent expression. "I can make biscuits, you know." She poured the eggs into a larger bowl filled with flour and mixed the ingredients until she had a ball of soft dough. "Occasionally my sisters would get out of the kitchen so I could have a turn."

"I'm looking forward to biscuits. Is Stuart up?"

She rolled the dough out on the counter. "I didn't hear anything from his room. Why was his knife found at the scene of the crime?"

"I'm going to find out."

"Honestly, the people in this house." She used a round cookie cutter and punched out the biscuits with more force than necessary.

"You know Stuart's harmless."

"Yes, but all this about stabbing and murder. Cam doesn't need the aggravation. He's anxious enough as it is about being a father."

There was plenty of coffee left, but I didn't see any evidence she was having a cup. "He'll be fine. So will you."

She gave me another suspicious look. "Thanks." She put the biscuits on a cookie sheet and put them in the oven. She wiped her hands on a dishcloth. "Any luck with Sean Snyder's case?"

"I don't have a lot to go on." I needed to find and talk to the elusive crystal seller, the knife seller, and all of Stuart's Klingon friends. I wanted to try for a look at the crime scene. I wanted a word with Eric O'Conner.

"It's odd there's been another murder in that hotel," Ellin said. "Maybe the same person killed Sean."

"That would be amazingly convenient."

By the time the biscuits were done Camden arrived home.

He gave Ellin a kiss. "Feel okay?"

"Of course." She wasn't about to let mere morning sickness slow her down. "Sorry I missed your solo. How'd it go?"

"Fine. Mimosa said to tell you hello and to remind you of the circle meeting Wednesday night."

"You told her I don't have time for that, I hope."

"She's just trying to include you, honey."

Ellin didn't really want to become involved in Camden's church. It wasn't narrow enough for her. "Well, tell her thank you for the offer, but no, thanks." She stacked the biscuits on a plate. "Would you take these to the table?"

Camden carried the plate of biscuits to the dining room table. I brought a bag of chips. Ellin dug in the fridge for butter, cheese, and jam. Camden got a Coke for himself and tea for Ellin. Kary came in as we were sitting down, so I fixed two glasses of iced tea and put one at her place.

Camden set a stack of paper napkins on the table. "I'll go see if Stuart wants lunch."

"Cam, you didn't see anything in Stuart's future about this?" Kary asked.

"Unfortunately, all I saw was something bad happening to Iris Hudson."

"She didn't listen to you?"

"She didn't want to listen to anyone." He went around through the island to the stairs.

Ellin reached for a biscuit. "He never had this problem until you moved in, Randall."

"Oh, I think he did."

After a few minutes, Camden came back to the table. "Stuart's okay. He just needed to sleep after that rough night. He wants to go back to the convention, but I don't think that's a good idea."

"He's going to stay here," Kary said in her best Teacher Voice. "I'll ask him to help grade some papers. He always enjoys that." She pointed her biscuit at me in a warning manner. "But I am definitely working on this case."

"Of course." I thought of something else. I took out my phone. "I'll text you the list of Stuart's Klingon friends. You can use my account and do a background check on them. Check for criminal records and any connections to Iris Hudson."

"Are you going back to the convention today?" Ellin asked.

I took another biscuit. "If it's open."

Kary passed Camden the chips. "So the murderer could be anyone at ExtravaganzaCon."

"That's possible," he said.

Ellin kept her glare. "Of course something will happen, Randall. Something always happens."

"And we always prevail, right, Camden?"

"That's because we are—" he paused for dramatic effect and I joined him.

"The Galaxy Kings!"

Ellin was not impressed. "If the convention's open, I suppose you're going to stay all day?"

"Come with us," Camden said.

"No," she said. "You two Galaxy Kings go. I have to work on the guest list for next month."

"Honey, it's Sunday. Take a break. If you come to the convention, you'll meet all kinds of interesting people who'd be perfect guests for the PSN."

"It's a science fiction convention, isn't it?" she said. "Not exactly psychic material."

"It's an everything convention," he said. "Multi-genre. UFOs, ghosts, Tarot cards, werewolves, vampires, you name it."

"And loads of people walking around in outlandish costumes."

"They're not all like that. Look at me."

She laughed. "Yes, look at you, Star Man."

When Ellin laughs, she really is incredibly attractive. Camden rubbed his forehead. "Is it still there?"

"Just a little. It looks like you've won a prize."

"First place for good behavior."

After lunch I went to my office and called the hotel. The convention would open at three.

"Time for the Galaxy Kings to get a move on," I said.

***

It had occurred to me that even though Eric O'Conner lived in Parkland, he might have checked into the Hilton, so the first thing I did upon arrival was to check with the hotel manager to ask for names and room numbers of the guests as part of my investigation into the deaths of Sean Snyder and Iris Hudson. No one under the name of O'Conner was listed.

The Enforcettes, in full battle array, met us in the lobby. Tiger caught Camden up and gave him a hug that took his breath away.

"Hello, your highness. How are you today?"

"I'm fine, thanks," he said when he was able.

"Somebody told us you were psychic. Is that true?"

"Yes," he said.

"Are you really?" Dawn said. "Why didn't you say so? That's so neat. I believe in reincarnation. I really believe I was Marie Curie."

Brianna looked at him with intent green eyes. "So have you been able to see who killed Iris Hudson?"

"I wish I could, but everything surrounding her is very cloudy. That usually means I'm involved somehow. I never see my own future."

"Does that mean you killed her?" Tiger asked. "The world owes you a debt of gratitude."

"Fortunately, I was with you when she was murdered."

"So you didn't like her, either?" I asked.

Tiger grimaced. "She accused us of pandering to men's baser instincts."

Dawn readjusted her tiny halter top. "Are you talking about that really rude woman who sneered at us?"

"That's the one."

"Oh, yeah, the Cosmic Cow."

"We'll help you," Brianna said. "Tell us what to do."

"Almost everyone was at the cosplay contest when she was killed," I said, "but if you find anyone who was on the eighth floor between eight and ten, they might have seen or heard something."

"We can do that." Dawn's eyes got big. "Gosh, suppose a serial killer is stalking the con? That'd make a great series, wouldn't it? KillerCon."

Tiger smiled. "You'll have to excuse Dawn. She's taken a few too many blows to the head."

Dawn objected to this. "It's your fault for hitting so hard."

"You're supposed to duck, silly."

"You're supposed to warn me."

"What's going on at the convention today?" I asked before their argument escalated into more blows to the head.

"There's been a lot of talk about two murders happening in the same hotel," Tiger said. "Someone's already come up with a theory that the hotel's haunted."

"Or the killer came through a rip in the time-space continuum," Brianna said.

"It's KillerCon," Dawn said. "I told you."

Tiger gave her a look. "The police took over one of the event rooms and have started interviewing people. It's put a damper on things, but everything will be back up to speed soon. We'll start asking around. Come on, girls."

"I'm going to retrace Stuart's steps," Camden said. "Maybe I'll zero in on something."

I went to have a talk with the knife salesman.

***

Aside from an area dedicated to fighting demonstrations, the Azalea Room was crowded with tables and booths devoted to SF warfare. Weapons of all shapes and sizes were hanging from partitions, spread out in rows, and crammed in boxes. I asked around until I found the dealer who'd sold Stuart his Pik-Ra knife. He was a large man, his baldness compensated by a long ponytail, sideburns, and a long mustache. He had on a black tee shirt decorated with Celtic symbols, heavy silver rings shaped like crosses, and a silver ankh dangling from one ear. He had all the religious bases covered.

He gave me a suspicious look out from under heavy eyebrows. "You a cop? I've already talked to enough cops."

"Licensed detective. I'm trying to piece together Saturday night's events," I said. "Stuart King's a friend of mine, so I'd appreciate it if you could tell me about your interactions with him."

"King was in here with a bunch of Klingons. He liked the knife. He bought it. I put his name on it. End of story, as far as I'm concerned."

The seller's table was covered with black cloth. Knives with decorative handles were laid out to show their designs, such as black widow spiders in their webs or patterns of skulls. Smaller pocket knives rested in a glass case. A larger case displayed long knives, daggers, and swords. The seller pointed out that the knives locked in the glass cases were real.

"Do you always deal in real knives?" I asked.

He sat down on the stool behind his display table. "Got a permit and everything. We had things cleared with the convention weeks in advance."

"Do you recall who was around when Stuart bought the knife?"

"I wasn't all that busy Saturday. Most people were getting ready for the costume contest."

"Did you go to the contest?"

"No, I stayed here."

"Any customers during the contest?"

"A few. Nobody else bought a Pik-Ra knife, though. King bought the last one."

"And you engraved his name on the handle."

"Yep, with this." He picked up a hand tool that looked like a small fat drill. "Doesn't take long." He pointed to a row of lethal-looking knives. "Now these I got in yesterday."

I picked one up. It was made of thick rubber.

At my questioning look, the knife seller said, "I'm not handling any more real ones, not at this con, anyway."

I set the knife back on the table. "Do you get many orders for real ones?"

"Most people are happy with plastic. Not as heavy."

"But Stuart wanted a real one?"

"I don't know. I had one Pik-Ra knife left, and it happened to be a real one. Too bad for Hudson, huh?"

If Stuart had only settled for another type of knife, something harmless, the murderer wouldn't have bothered to steal it and use it on Iris Hudson.

"I take it you weren't a fan?" I asked.

"Oh, her books are okay, but she's a pain—was a pain. I was set up near book signings at TransPlanetaryCon last April and never heard such bitching in my life. I'm writing my own series of alternate universe novels, and if I ever get famous and have my own book signings, you'd better believe I'll be real nice to whoever buys my books. Why didn't her agent or publishing house just hire somebody to impersonate her? The real Iris Hudson could've stayed home if she hated cons so much."

"Too late now." I looked through his supply, checking for real knives with serrated edges. "When did you get to the con?"

"We got in Friday night and set up then."

"Anybody buy anything then?"

"We weren't open till Saturday."

"You're not missing any knives?"

"Cops asked me the same thing. The Friday murder, right? All my knives were accounted for. I double checked. Besides, from what they told me, that Snyder fellow was killed with a different kind of knife from what I sell."

"Some kind of butcher knife?"

"The way they described it, I'd say it was more specialized." He reached behind the table, pulled out a huge catalog, and flipped through the pages. I never realized there were that many knives in the world. He found the page he wanted. "Here. Something like this."

He turned the catalog so I could see. The knives on both pages were small but wicked-looking, with smooth handles and serrated edges. "What would you use this kind of knife for?"

He shrugged. "Most anything. Camping, sailing, cut rope, gut fish, stab people. I don't deal in them because they're too ordinary looking for the SF crowd."

"But it would be very easy for anyone to get a knife like this."

"Too easy, and you know there are a lot of nutcases out there."

A man who looked like a mutant Atilla the Hun came up to the table. "Ho, there! What have you got in the way of a soul-sucking Gardonian battle-axe?"

The knife seller gave me a look as if to say, "See what I mean?"

CHAPTER TEN

"The Dark Crystal"

Even though Iris Hudson wasn't well-liked, her books were landmark creations in science fiction, so I was a little surprised to find the con humming along as if nothing had happened only an hour after re-opening. The police continued their interviews, but neither that nor the fact there had been two murders in two days seemed to bother the convention-goers. Other officers roamed the halls and the dealers' room, otherwise, it was business as usual. A tribute for Hudson to be held at four thirty in the Longleaf Room had been hastily scheduled.

I paused at the *Galaxy Kings* display, the TV show I had enjoyed so much when I was eight—a strange mix of science fiction and fantasy. Two kings from two different planets joined forces to fight their enemies, a race of man-eating creatures, the worst one being Gorbo, a monkey-like thing with a fixed grin and the unnerving habit of jumping out of the dark when least expected. I recalled many a Friday night waiting with a tight stomach for Gorbo to make an appearance, never guessing when he'd show up, and leaping for safety behind my father's chair. My dad would laugh and say, "It's just a guy in an ape suit, for crying out loud."

I looked up at the life-sized Gorbo. How had this managed to scare me? It was really hokey-looking.

Camden came up to the display. "Still scares me."

"Nah, look. You can see the zipper."

"I watched one too many episodes. You remember the one when they were lost in the caves on Quantax Four?"

A particularly dark and chilling episode.

"Branton thought Chase was right behind him, and it was Gorbo? You could see that awful grin in the half-light, but Branton couldn't see it."

One of my best leaps behind the chair. "I was yelling at the screen: 'Look out! He's behind you!'"

"I was curled in a fetal ball in my room at Mrs. Camden's."

I thought of how my dad had laughed and shouted warnings to the oblivious Galaxy King, of how he'd said, "Now you watch, Davey. Branton has to get away. The Kings have to be back next week for another adventure."

Camden hadn't had any such comfort. He'd probably been watching all by himself in the dark upstairs room of his foster home, his imagination set on high and his psychic powers sending him even more frightening images.

I gave the Gorbo a poke with my finger. "Want to knock it over?"

He looked around. The dealers' room wasn't too crowded, and nobody was paying us any attention.

"We could say it was an accident."

I could tell the idea was appealing, but he shook his head. "Find out anything from the knife salesman?"

"Nothing I can use right now. How about you?"

"There have been too many convention-goers in the halls and in and out of the hospitality room for me to pick up anything useful."

I checked my watch. "There's a service of sorts for Hudson in half an hour. I'm hoping to talk to Hudson's manager if he's there. Meanwhile let's see if the crystal seller showed up."

Back in the dealers' room, Princess Leia's neighbor had indeed shown up and spread chunks of crystal all over his table. He also had crystal pendants, bracelets, and earrings on display, as well as a selection of books with titles like, *Crystal Healing For Beginners* and *Find Your Personal Power Through Crystals*. The dealer was a medium-sized man with a cloud of wispy white hair and a mild expression.

I thought Bob Plank was a curiously solid name for a man who looked as if he might float away. "Oh, good, you're here," I said. "I want to buy a crystal for a friend of mine."

He beamed at me, either from joy at fulfilling my wish or the idea of making a sale. "I'm sure we can find exactly the right one. What's your friend's primary color, do you know?"

"Red. Bright red."

"And his—excuse me," he said to Camden. "This is remarkable. Do you know you bear a striking resemblance to the crystal spirit in Touringdale's *Life Within the Light*?"

"Apparently, I look like a lot of things," Camden said.

"You must have an unusually brilliant aura."

I grinned at Camden. "I've always thought so."

"I'm sorry," Bob Plank said. "Getting back to your friend. I think he'll enjoy this fine crystal." He picked up a large piece of sparkly rock and handed it to me. "You see the garnet crystals embedded in the very heart? A powerful stone."

I didn't have any trouble admiring the rock. "This is very nice. What do you think, Camden? Would Geoff like this?"

Camden played along. "Geoff Snyder? He might."

"Geoff Snyder?" Plank snatched the rock from my hand. "There's no way you're giving any of my crystals to Geoff Snyder."

"What's wrong?" I asked.

Plank quivered with indignation. "That man and his brother nearly ruined me. I was all set to go on a twenty-city tour to promote my book, *Crystal Cures*, when they dared me to prove my claims. I was so upset by their accusations I couldn't travel. It took weeks to recover. You're friends of his?"

"More like acquaintances," I said. Apparently, the news of Sean Snyder's murder hadn't reached Plank. "When did that happen?"

"Six months ago. I can't tell you the sales I lost by not going on that tour."

"But you're doing okay here, aren't you?"

"We'll see. I just got here. I've never understood why some people feel the need to ruin things for other people. They don't have to believe in the power of crystals, but they sure as hell don't have to force their misguided belief on everyone else."

I got the impression this was one of the few times Bob Plank had been riled enough to say "hell." "Did you confront them about this?"

"Oh, no. I didn't want to be anywhere near them."

"But you said they dared you to prove crystals can heal."

"On television. They were on a local morning show talking about all aspects of the paranormal and how everything was a sham. Then they started talking about me. I was appalled."

"Why didn't you call the station and ask for equal time to express your views?"

"I was crushed. I took to my bed. I tell you it took me weeks to get over that. I was called out on Facebook and Twitter, and some of my buyers dropped me."

I really wanted to say, why didn't you heal yourself? "Why didn't you contact the Snyders?"

"I did! I sent them several pithy emails telling them they had no right to destroy other peoples' faith. They didn't have the courtesy to reply."

Pithy. I glanced at Camden. There was a word you didn't hear every day.

"I'm sorry to hear about that."

"I'll be glad to sell you a crystal as long as none of my treasures end up in Geoff Snyder's hands."

"See anything you like, Camden?"

Camden carefully touched each crystal. Apparently none of Plank's treasures had any harmful vibes. "We heard you have a wonderful selection. We looked for you yesterday. Did you have some trouble getting to the convention?"

"My flight was delayed in Chicago. The weather's been pretty bad up there. Timmy and I spent the night at the airport."

For a moment I thought he might be talking about a pet crystal, but he pointed to a pretty young woman a few aisles over. She had on a tutu and fairy wings.

"Such a sweetheart." He gave her a little wave and she waved back. "My niece. It's her first con. Her first airplane ride. There's her mother, that woman over there in the cat suit."

A cat suit that was stretched to its limits. Well, there was his alibi.

Camden set a blue crystal aside. "I may come back for this one."

"Take your time deciding. I have plenty more like it."

Plank's fairy niece twirled by as Camden and I went back up the aisle.

"Even without the alibi, if that guy couldn't even rouse himself to call the TV station and protest, I don't think he'd stick a knife in Sean Snyder," I said.

"It doesn't seem likely."

I gave Geoff Snyder a call to tell him Bob Plank had arrived, but had an alibi.

Geoff was no longer interested in Bob Plank. "What the hell is going on in this hotel? They moved me to the tenth floor, and now I hear there's been another murder not far from where Sean and I were staying on the eighth. I am checking out as soon as possible."

So much for the Parkland Hilton's reputation.

"Camden said the killer was someone Sean knew. But neither of us knew Iris Hudson! It doesn't make sense."

"No, it doesn't," I said. "But if there's a connection, I'll find it."

"What can I do to help?"

"Have you been through all of your social media? There could be an angry comment or threat I missed." Or that you blocked, I might have said.

"All comments are positive," he said, "but I'll look back through the archives just in case."

He ended the call. I took another glance at my watch. "Let's go see who's decided to come pay their respects to Iris Hudson."

CHAPTER ELEVEN

"Things To Come"

Howerver heart-broken he might have been by the death of his client, Vincent Parnell was hiding it well. We found him in the Longleaf Room, enjoying the temporary limelight as he spoke about Hudson.

"The world has lost a shining star in the literary firmament. Iris Hudson's work was as far-reaching, brilliant, and lyrical as anything written by Asimov, Clarke, or Bradbury."

All the seats were filled, so Camden and I leaned against the back wall with the overflow crowd as Parnell continued to compare Iris to every science-fiction author on the planet. He finally finished his remarks.

"I know we can't truly express how we feel at this sad time, so I'd like to ask for a few moments of silence in Iris's memory." After a suitable time, he said, "Thank you. If anyone has anything they'd like to say, please come forward."

I hoped someone might leap up and shout, "I did it!" but this didn't happen. Several fans went up to the podium. Each one told how Hudson's work had inspired them, or thrilled them, or encouraged them, how her stories had helped them through bad times, or made them feel they weren't alone in the universe, or taught them to reach for their dreams, that Love Conquers All.

The final speaker was Thomas Warburn, the actor who'd played

Captain Clark in *Beyond the Asteroids*, a TV show my fifteen-year old self thought was the coolest ever. The man was in his sixties, fit and square-jawed as ever, his sandy hair only slightly gray.

"This is indeed a sad day," he said. He paused to give one of his trademark long looks around the room. "A sad day. Iris Hudson will be remembered not only for the wonderful books she has left us, but for her towering presence as a crusader for women writers of science fiction. I had the pleasure of working with Iris many years ago, and I was impressed by her fire and determination."

I tuned out the rest of his eulogy. "Did Iris do anything on *Beyond the Asteroids*?" I whispered to Camden.

"Not that I know of," he replied.

Warburn finished, and Parnell took his place. "Thank you, Mr. Warburn, for that fine tribute."

Someone in the crowd asked, "Did Ms. Hudson leave any unfinished manuscripts?"

"There are several finished manuscripts," Parnell said, and there was a murmur of excitement. "I'll have more information on that later."

At the end of the tribute, fans eagerly snatched up their choices from a large stack of Hudson's books. I picked up a copy of the second book in the *Dark Star* series, *Dark Territories*. Inside was Iris Hudson's trademark scrawl. At least it looked like the same scrawl. I was sure Parnell had mastered it, just as he'd mastered the fine art of spinning.

Camden and I waited until the fans were gone and Parnell was counting up all the cash and checks before we approached him. Camden went first.

"Mr. Parnell, my sympathies." He offered his hand, and Parnell shook it. "I am a huge fan of Iris's work, and I appreciate the wonderful things you said about her."

"Thank you."

Camden gave me a slight nod and moved aside.

"Mr. Parnell, if I might have a moment. My name is David Randall. I'm investigating the murder of Iris Hudson."

He paused in his counting. "I don't recall hiring any investigators."

"I'm here on behalf of Stuart King."

"Isn't that convenient? The murderer sends his own detective. How thoughtful."

"Stuart didn't kill Iris."

"You may believe what you wish, Mr. Randall. I saw him skulking around the hallway, looking at all the doors, trying to find her room. Now that I think of it, I'm probably responsible for him finding her. He gave me a guilty look when I came out of her room."

"Did he stay in the hall?"

"No. He scuttled away while I was waiting for the elevator."

"So you think he came back, somehow got into Ms Hudson's locked room, and killed her?"

"Do you have a better explanation?"

"Where did you go next?"

He drew himself up, insulted. "I went to the authors' roundtable and sat in for Ms. Hudson. It lasted until almost ten. You can check with the organizers. I would've gotten back to her room sooner, but there was some sort of commotion in the lobby, people racing about like wild things, screaming and shouting."

Eric O'Conner's bid to become Jerk of the Con.

Parnell's eyes were hard. "Do you think I killed her?"

I gave Camden a quick glance. He shook his head. "I have no reason to think so. Did she talk to you like she talked to those people in line?"

"I won't pretend we were great friends, but we had an excellent business relationship. We worked well together. She did the writing, and I handled everything else." He put the cash and checks into a pouch and picked up the two remaining copies of *Dark Star Two: Dark Territories.* "If you don't mind."

"One other thing. Given her well-known reputation, why would she open the door for Stuart?"

For the first time, he looked disconcerted. "I don't know. Perhaps she thought it was me. Perhaps he disguised his voice."

"Do you know if Ms. Hudson had any interactions with Sean and Geoff Snyder?"

"Snyder? Wasn't the other man who was killed named Snyder?"

"Yes."

"Why would she know them?"

"They're also authors."

"I don't know."

"You'll be going through her things, won't you? Her papers and manuscripts? If you find anything relating to the Snyders, let me know."

"Why should I?"

"Because I want to find out who killed her, and so do you. She may have been a thoughtless and unkind woman, but nobody deserves to die like that."

He gave me a long stare, his mouth trembled a little, and then he said, "You're right. I don't think there's any connection, but I'll look."

***

Camden and I left the Longleaf Room and made our way through a hallway crowded with Transformers, Wonder Women, and three people dressed as the little alien toys from *Toy Story*. For once, no one remarked that Camden looked like someone or something else.

"Speaking of connections," I said, "what's the connection between Parnell and Iris? If she was that disagreeable, why would he want to work with her? The pay must have been awfully good."

"He said they had an excellent business relationship and worked well together."

"There might be something else."

"He didn't kill her."

"He could've arranged her murder, ever think of that?"

"I didn't get that impression, either."

The Enforcettes flagged us down at the corner.

"Sorry we haven't been able to come up with any clues," Tiger said. "The only people we found who are staying on the eighth floor have rooms way down the hall from Hudson's, and they were all at the cosplay contest. But we reported the theft of our trophy to the con organizers and they've banned O'Conner from the con, so we did get that accomplished."

"Well, that won't keep him away," Brianna said. "He'll just put on one of his stupid disguises and fake his way back in."

"But we know all his stupid disguises," Dawn said. "We'll find some way to catch him."

"That's the plan," Brianna said. "You guys in?"

"You bet," I said, "but we're heading home. We'll join you tomorrow."

***

On our way home, we stopped by Chunky Chicken and got sandwiches and fries for everyone. We found Kary and Stuart sitting at the dining room table, a big stack of school papers between them.

Kary brightened when she saw the Chunky Chicken bags. "Good timing, guys. Stuart and I just finished, and he was wondering what to make for supper." She pushed the stack aside. "I'll fix drinks."

I put the bags on the kitchen counter, and Camden pulled out paper plates from one of the cabinets. "You okay, Stuart?" he asked.

"I'm okay. But gosh, I wish I'd never bought that Pik-Ra knife!"

Kary filled four glasses with ice and poured the tea. "I Googled the Klingons and cross-referenced them to Sean Snyder and Iris Hudson. Nothing. What about Geoff? As much as I hate to say it, family members are usually the prime suspects."

Camden set a sandwich and fries at her place. "Geoff didn't kill his brother."

"Then we're still at square one."

"I'm afraid so."

After eating only half of his sandwich, Stuart said he was tired and went upstairs. I remembered an unpleasant task. "I need to check in with your dad and give him his daily report," I said to Kary.

Kary opened a ketchup packet and squeezed the contents over her fries. "I'm sure he insisted on that."

"Help me think of something colorful to tell him."

"Tell him whatever you like."

"Let's see. Someone's been running around ExtravaganzaCon stabbing people with a large fantasy knife. I talked with the knife salesman and a crystal seller, then went to a service for the murdered author no one liked. I have yet to corner Eric O'Connor, who may or may not be the killer or the Angel of Truth. I'm hoping he's one and the same so I can tie things up neatly."

She reached for another packet. "Or you could say I'm in the midst of a murder investigation and your problem isn't worth spit. Notice I said 'spit' to be polite."

Camden angled his chicken sandwich for another bite. "I realize he deserves to be mocked, but hasn't this happened before? A ministry like his is just asking for it."

"I think the Angel of Truth is getting too close to the truth, or a truth my father doesn't want anyone to know."

After dinner, I called Pastor Gary and told him I had nothing new to report. He huffed and snorted and spouted some Bible verses about laziness and sloth and hung up. I took another look at the videos. The fake pastor was incoherent in most of them, but in one, the gibberish became unintelligible as "the sins of the fathers," which he repeated until he fake choked and started rolling on the floor.

Ellin had actually worked from home, so she, thanked Camden for the chicken sandwich, and turned the conversation to the topic of When Are You Coming to the Studio. Camden said he was going to check on Stuart, and escaped upstairs.

After a while, I went to the kitchen to refill my tea glass. Ellin was sitting by herself at the table, coffee cup in front of her on the placemat.

"That had better be milk in that cup," I said.

"Shut up." Her eyes and nose were red.

"Or maybe it's whiskey." A closer look revealed she'd been crying. This was so uncharacteristic I sat down across from her. "What's the matter?"

Sometimes she'll talk to me. I don't know why. She was tired, and I've inherited my bartender father's Tell Me All expression.

She gave a big sniff. "Randall, the only success I've ever had in my life is the PSN. I know a lot of people think it's a silly network, but I've brought it up from one show to three, and all three are doing well. In everything else, I've failed miserably. I don't want to fail with this baby."

"What makes you think you're going to fail?"

I thought she might be concerned about labor pains or swollen ankles, but Ellin was too tough to let little things like that slow her down.

"I haven't any motherly traits. I have no patience. I don't cook or sew or make little crafts. I'm going to be terrible."

"What would you have to cook? Baby food comes in jars. You don't have to sew, either. Baby clothes come ready-made these days. You can even buy little crafts if you need to."

"What the hell do you know about it?" She turned even redder and softened her tone. "Sorry, Randall."

"It's easy to forget," I said, "but I'm the only one in this house who's been a parent. It may not be much, but I'm willing to help."

She slumped in her chair. "I don't have time for a baby."

"Camden has time. I have time. You're always talking about how organized you are. Here's your chance to prove it. Work, home, family—she does it all. It's Super Ellin."

"I don't know. It's a huge responsibility."

"Nobody's ever been a parent before. You'll do some things right and some things wrong. But the baby will love you, no matter what."

She reached for her coffee cup, reconsidered, and let her hand drop in her lap. "I hope so."

"Look," I said, "you're one of the luckiest women alive. You have a husband who's willing to stay home and look after the baby so you can have your career. Do you know how many women would kill for this opportunity? Plus you have me, the built-in babysitter."

She gave me the eye. "I'm not sure what kind of influence you'll be on my child."

"I guess we'll find out, won't we?"

She didn't say anything for a while. Then she made a decision. "Randall, we've had our differences, but I can't deny you're Cam's best friend, and even when the pair of you go haring off to do God knows what, I can pretty well depend on you to bring him home in one piece. I can't deny your two-bit agency has actually helped people and solved crimes. But if you want to stay, then deal with whatever you're dealing with and stay."

What was I dealing with? It couldn't be the thought of Camden's baby. I was going to be the best damn Uncle Dave she ever had. Was I afraid another little girl was going to bring back too many memories? But I was handling all that, wasn't I?

I realized I'd been staring off into space. I came back to find Ellin's intense blue gaze looking right at me. She didn't say anything else. She left her cup on the table and went upstairs. I looked out at the dark backyard and tried to imagine a little blond girl playing there, but she continued to morph into a little girl with long brown curls and a white lace dress, the same little girl I dreamed about that night.

***

As always, Lindsey stood near the edge of a vast playground. I could make out misty shapes of seesaws and sliding boards and hear children's voices calling to each other. I hoped Iris Hudson wasn't in there trying to push kids off the swings.

A breeze I couldn't feel lifted the ribbons in Lindsey's hair and the lacy trim of her dress. *You shouldn't worry, Daddy. You fixed my bicycle. You taught me all those old songs. You took me to the circus and the zoo and to dance lessons every week. You can do those things with another baby. I believe you can do anything, even this.*

"I'm going to try," I said in the dream.

Can you help her, Daddy? Can you help the sad lady?

"You don't mean Kary, do you? Or, hard as it is for me to believe, Ellin? She was really sad for a while tonight."

No.

"Do you mean Iris? I'm going to find out who killed her."

No, not that one.

"Who is the sad lady, then? Is she with you?" I thought about Sean's dead wife. "Is her name Natalie? Is she sad because her husband was killed?"

No.

"What can you tell me about this other lady? Is she an artist? Is her name Leena?"

The dream began to fade. Beside me, Kary turned over and smacked my face with her elbow. Now I was definitely awake. But I wasn't concerned. Lindsey would contact me again, and I'd have another chance to figure out what she meant. What I remembered from the dream was much more important to me than finding a sad lady.

I believe you can do anything, even this.

CHAPTER TWELVE

"Journey to the Center of the Earth"

By the time I got up Monday morning, Ellin and Kary had already gone to work. As I staggered around the kitchen, making coffee and wondering how many cups Ellin had knocked back, I saw Camden in the backyard helping Buddy take some wood out of Buddy's pickup. Buddy is large and loud, so it wasn't hard to overhear him.

"Hang on a minute, Cam. That piece ain't cherry." He pulled another plank out of the truck. He saw me at the kitchen door and waved. "Mornin,' Randall."

"Good morning," I said. "What's with all the wood?"

"It's for a cradle," Camden said.

Buddy handed him the plank. "Found some real good pieces in my shop."

"Hear anything from Stuart this morning?" I asked Camden.

"He's deciding whether or not to go back to the convention. He's afraid it might look like he's returning to the scene of the crime."

"Well, we're all returning to the scene of the crime. I'm heading over to the convention to chat with the Klingons. You coming with me?"

"Buddy's going to help me get started on the cradle," Camden said. "Then he can give me a ride."

"Me and Rufus is going over there to do some gaming," Buddy said. "Won't be no problem."

"Okay," I said. "See you guys there."

***

When I arrived at the convention center at ten, ExtravaganzaCon was in full swing. It was easy to find the Klingons. They were clustered in a noisy group by the *Star Trek* exhibit, getting their books signed by an actor who'd played a Klingon officer in one of the movies. They tried their throat-clearing language on me, but I wasn't in the mood to play.

"Cut the gargling and listen up. I need some info. Who was with Stuart Saturday when he bought the Pik-Ra knife?"

Three of them raised their hands.

"Tell me about the purchase."

"The guy said it was the last Pik-Ra he had," a man said. "Stuart asked how much, and then he bought it. No big deal."

"So the three of you knew he had a real knife?"

The group exchanged glances and nodded. "Yeah," one said. "We didn't think anything of it. It was a cool-looking knife."

Another man said, "We all had a look at it, and then Stuart put it in his bag, and we went to the initiation ceremony."

"He took the knife out for the ceremony, right? Did any of you see it after that? In the food court, maybe, or the art room?"

The Kingons all agreed the last time they saw Stuart's knife was during their initiation ceremony.

"Which one of you is Shannon?" I asked. They all looked alike in their turtle heads.

A shorter Klingon raised her hand. "That's me."

"Could I speak to you for a minute, please?" I led Shannon over away from the others. "Stuart says you invited him to your room, but he couldn't find it. Can you explain what happened?"

Underneath her alien makeup, she blushed. "Oh, gosh, I was so embarrassed. You see, I thought Stuart was Justin."

"Justin?"

"That guy over there."

Justin was another short, round Klingon. In full Klingon costume, he and Stuart could easily have been mistaken for one another.

"I was really interested in Justin, and when I realized I'd been talking to Stuart instead, I gave him the wrong room number. It was mean of me, I know, but I was sort of flustered."

"So you didn't see Stuart at all that night."

"No. After we left the art room, I met Justin at the crafts section, ballroom C, and we, well, you know."

I glanced back at Justin "Okay, thanks."

There were lots of Vulcans and Borg, and after a lot of dead ends, I found the ones who were with Stuart when he took the elevator from the eighth floor down to the cosplay event at about eight PM. I introduced myself and explained I was investigating Iris Hudson's murder. The Vulcans and Borg had traveled to the convention from Florida and had adjoining rooms on the eighth floor, Iris Hudson's hall. They told me they'd been heading down to the cosplay contest when a fellow dressed as the Green Hornet rushed by in a big hurry, knocking over a smaller than average Klingon waiting at the elevator.

Stuart had failed to mention this. The Green Hornet, aka Eric O'Conner. Running late to ruin the Enforcettes' skit?

"Did you see the Green Hornet take anything from the Klingon's bag?" I asked.

"No," one Vulcan said. "He just charged on."

The Borg didn't speak, but nodded their agreement, their home made costumes creaking.

"Was anyone else in the hallway at that time?" I asked.

"There was a Druid also waiting, as I recall," the Vulcan said. "Tall fellow, all in a gray robe and hood."

Druids were harder to find. I finally saw a lean fellow in a white robe and hood who said yes, he was a Druid, and no, he hadn't been in the hallway of the eighth floor or in the elevator Saturday night at 8. He and his fellow Druids were staying on the fifth floor.

"How many Druids are here?" I asked.

"Eleven, and that evening we were all at a symposium on the Mysteries of Stonehenge."

Of course. "Do all of you dress in the white robes?"

"Standard Druid issue."

"So, not gray. Would anyone else be wearing a similar costume?"

He chuckled. "You do understand this is a science fiction and fantasy convention, right? There are a lot of people in cloaks and hoods. Elves, hobbits, travelers, foresters, you name it."

Great, I thought. Thanks for narrowing it down.

***

In the dealers' room, the Enforcettes were signing autographs for their fans and having their pictures taken with eager teenage boys.

Brianna pushed the next boy away and came to me. "What do you think about all of us fanning out and seeing if we can spot O'Connor?"

"Brianna," I said, "can't you get a restraining order or something?"

She raised her eyebrows. "Randall. To prevent the man from ruining our science fiction cosplay? Nobody would take that seriously."

"We'd all like to catch him," Tiger said.

"I've been by his house," I said. "It looks deserted. Any idea where he might be? He's not registered at the hotel."

"Oh, he's way too cheap to stay at the Hilton," Brianna said. "He's probably crashing with one of his video game pals."

"Does he always work alone?"

"Yes," she said.

I scanned the crowd. "You'd think he'd be here."

"Oh, he probably is. We just can't see him. Once we pose for a few more pictures and sign some autographs, we should start hunting for him, what do you say?"

"I'm in," I said.

I didn't see O'Conner, but I saw Rufus, Buddy, and Camden coming down the aisle. Rufus used to live with us at 302 Grace, but moved out when he and his wife Angie found a house they liked two streets over. Rufus and Buddy were typical Good Old Boys, which is a Southern expression for large easy-going men who look slow and stupid but are deceptively clever. Rufus was taller than Buddy, with red hair tied back in a braid that stuck out from under his baseball cap and a scraggly red beard. Buddy had on his overalls, and Rufus wore jeans and an X-Men tee shirt.

Camden was stopped by a tall young woman dressed as Dot the android from *Spaceballs*.

"Excuse me," she said. "Aren't you the one who was the Star Prince in a skit last night? Do you remember an episode of *The War for the Island Planet*, the one with the king who loved clocks and turned out to be a clockwork creature himself? You look just like him. What was his name? Noel something. Really, it's remarkable."

Buddy gave a snort. "He don't look like no clock."

Camden started to thank him when Rufus said, "He's a dead ringer for Alan in *Zero Darkness*."

"I don't believe I know that show," the woman said.

"That's because it's a game. Look it up sometime. You'll see I'm right. Spitting image." He stopped and gave the Enforcettes a long whistle. "Well, butter my butt and call me a biscuit if it ain't the Enforcettes!" Rufus touched the brim of his cap. "Pleased to meet you ladies. Mighty nice costumes."

"Thanks," Tiger said. "You guys look like you wandered over from *Texas Chainsaw Massacre*."

"Naw, we always look like this. You gals have made my day. Say hello to the Enforcettes, Bud! You don't often get to meet the hottest babes in the galaxy."

Buddy wiped his hand on his overalls before offering it to the women. "You three look hotter than Satan's housecat."

The Enforcettes were either Southern women or had lived in the South long enough to appreciate some of the more peculiar sayings. "We sure do," Dawn said.

Rufus turned to me. "Randall, what's this business about a murder? Stuart's all upset. What'd he do?"

The Enforcettes were called away by another group of eager young men with cameras and autograph books. "Not much. Ended up in the wrong place trying to score with a female Klingon, but she purposely gave him the wrong room number."

"Damn shifty Kingons."

"He's not under suspicion," I said. "I want to talk to a man named Eric O'Conner., who is also Brianna's ex and a known troublemaker. I'd like to find out if there's some connection between him and Iris. As soon as the Enforcettes finish with their fans, we're starting our hunt."

"We can help you look for him."

"Weren't we gonna go see *Fatal Fantasy*?" Buddy asked.

"We can do that later."

"Yeah, but I ain't seen it in a while. It's a damn good movie," he said to us. "This astronaut finds out this world she thought was real ain't real, and there's these fish critters she's crazy about, only they turn out to be star people and she kills them so nobody else gets caught up in the fantasy and then finds out they was gonna save the Earth—come to think of it, Cam, you kinda look like one of them star people. Their eyes wasn't as big as yours, though."

"They don't need to hear the whole dang movie, Bud," Rufus said. "They've seen every old sci-fi movie there is. And we don't need to see it again. When else are you gonna get the chance to help out the Enforcettes?"

The Enforcettes came back, fired up and ready for action. "Okay, boys, let's go get him."

I gave Rufus and Buddy O'Conner's description. "He's about my height, brown hair, and dressed either as the Green Hornet or Indiana Jones."

"Or Batman," Brianna said. "Or Ironman, or some weird superhero he made up named Gorp or something.

"Are you sure that's all?" I asked.

"All I know of," she said, and we split up to begin our search.

I went up to the third floor to the hospitality room and talked to the people there. "Were any of you here around eight or eight thirty last night? There was a Doctor Who, some Andorans, and some lizard people."

They shook their heads.

"Anybody on duty in here, or do you just wander in and out?"

"There are some hotel staff members keeping an eye on

things," a woman dressed as Fiona from *Shrek* told me.

No one was keeping an eye at the moment, so I took another trip down to the front desk. The same helpful young man was there. "I've got another question," I said. Who was on duty Saturday night in the third floor hospitality room?"

He checked his computer. "Kenna. She won't be in until after lunch."

"She's working there again?"

"Yes, she'll be here at the desk until four, and then she takes a dinner break and works the hospitality room six to ten."

I thanked him and met Camden and the Enforcettes back at the food court. No one had had any luck.

"Maybe he won't come back," Dawn said.

Brianna rolled her eyes. "Of course he will. He can't stand to be out of the action for long."

"Maybe Rufus and Buddy found him," Camden said.

I scanned the crowd for baseball caps. "In that case, there might not be much left. Oh, there's Rufus." I waved him over.

Rufus had bought some buttons to go on his tee shirt. One was the logo for the lizard drama, *V*, and one said "I Died and Went to Thanksgiving," which was a reference to an episode of *MacGyver*. "You have any idea how many Batmans are in this crowd?" Rufus said. "Me and Bud scared the hell out of most of 'em, but none was O'Conner."

"Startled a few Indiana Joneses, too," Buddy said with a grin. "Didn't see no Green Hornets, though, and the one Ironman walking around is about four feet tall."

"We really appreciate your help," Brianna said.

"No trouble at all," he said. "Me and Buddy's gonna play some *Alien Death Race,* but we'll keep an eye out for him. You ladies don't have some buttons from your show, do you?"

"You can get buttons and posters from the dealer on aisle fifteen," Tiger said. "Come on, we'll show you."

"We'll even sign the poster," Dawn said.

"Ladies, that'd be better than a six pack on Christmas."

"Now there's a picture," I said to Camden as Rufus escorted the Enforcettes out of the food court. "Looks like an especially weird cross-over. Tonight, on channel 12, *The Enforcettes, Voyage to the Redneck Planet*. You want to grab something to eat here?"

"Yeah, that sounds good." He paused. "Stuart's here."

Sure enough, a short round Klingon came cautiously down the aisle as if expecting an attack from the Federation at any minute.

"Stuart, over here," Camden called.

Stuart scurried to us. His head piece was slightly askew and wobbled when he wiped his forehead. "Whew! I wasn't sure this was a good idea, but I hated to miss the convention today. I'd already asked for the day off from Super Food." He looked around furtively. "Nobody'll know it's me, though, will they?"

"The perfect disguise," I said. "Come have some lunch with us."

We found a table at the food court and ordered Cosmic Combos: cheeseburgers, fries, and colas in tall cups with PanGalactic GargleBlaster logos.

Stuart settled in his chair and took a long drink of his GargleBlaster. "You guys have any luck this morning?"

I took a handful of fries. "No. Clear some things up for me. You and Parnell saw each other in the hallway. That's it?"

"He glared at me and I left. I didn't think anything of it."

"So what's this about the Green Hornet trying to run you over at the elevator? You left out that part before."

"Oh, yeah."

I had to wait until Stuart swallowed his bite of cheeseburger before he continued.

"I was waiting for the elevator with the Borg and Vulcans, and this guy in a trench coat and hat ran into me. I thought at first he was Inspector Gadget, but then I saw his mask and knew he was the Green Hornet. He bumped into me, and I landed on a Borg. He apologized."

"The guy who bumped you or the Borg?"

"The Borg. The Green Hornet ran on down the hall. Like he was late for something."

"Stuart, why didn't you mention this before? I'm thinking this guy is the man who caused all the fuss with the Enforcettes. Do you remember anything else about him?"

Stuart thought a while. It was going to be too much to expect him to say, Oh, yes, and he had a distinctive snake tattoo on his left cheek, he favored his left leg, and he smelled like shoe polish.

Stuart shook his head. "Sorry, Randall. I was in his way, he ran into me, he ran off down the hall. That's it."

"He'd been coming from which direction?"

"Down the same hallway."

"From Iris Hudson's room?"

"Yeah."

"Okay, let me try to get it straight," I said. "After snubbing you, Antenna Woman, and the Green Hornet, Iris goes to her room around five thirty. Parnell is the last one to see her alive, around eight. He sees Stuart bumbling around looking for Shannon's room. For some reason, O'Conner is also on the eighth floor and runs into Stuart before getting away. Parnell comes back at ten. Iris doesn't answer the door or his phone call, so he gets security to open the door, and finds Iris stabbed to death. We don't know exactly when she was killed, but if Parnell saw her alive at eight and discovered her body after the Authors' Roundtable at ten, she must have been killed between, say, eight-fifteen and ten, when practically everyone was at the cosplay contest."

Camden wasn't convinced. "But how would O'Conner get Stuart's knife? Unless he's some sort of magician, he couldn't have taken anything from Stuart's bag without one of the Vulcans noticing. Did the Green Hornet touch your bag, Stuart?"

"I don't think so."

"Stuart last saw his knife during the initiation ceremony from five to six," Camden said. "O'Conner would have had to steal it after that. Do you remember seeing the Green Hornet in the food court when you had your Battle Feast, Stuart?"

"Uh, no."

"How about in the art room when you went to see Shannon's portrait of Worf?"

He shook his head. "There were a lot of people in both places."

"Stuart, the only time you remember putting your bag down is in the hospitality room, correct?" I asked.

"That's right," Stuart said.

"What time was that?"

"Oh, I guess eight fifteen or so."

"And how long did you stay?"

"Maybe twenty minutes. I wanted to see some of the cosplay contest."

"So you might have had your knife when you got to the hospitality room. Did you look in your bag when you left?"

There was a long pause that told me no, he didn't. "I don't remember," he said.

"The murderer could've gotten it then. I'll talk with Kenna, the woman who was working in the hospitality room between six and ten last night. But it's a long shot."

Camden didn't think this was probable, either. "You think O'Conner is a suspect?"

"Maybe."

"So when he ran into Stuart, he saw the knife in his bag and somehow knew Stuart would be in the hospitality room around eight, stole the knife, went back up to the eighth floor, found a way into Iris's room, what, around nine, maybe? Killed her, and then dashed back downstairs to steal Brianna's trophy after the cosplay contest ended at ten?"

"What do you and your superpowers think?"

"Well, I don't know. I told you everything was cloudy. But my regular powers think it's highly unlikely to me O'Conner's the killer."

I shook out the last fry from the container. "Speaking of cloudy, Camden, do you have any idea what Lindsey means by the sad lady?"

He and I had an odd psychic connection, so he was in tune with Lindsey. "My best guess would be Iris Hudson."

"Nope. And it's not Sean's wife either. I think it's Leena Fay, the artist, but I have no idea how I can help her. She's expected today."

"You'll figure it out," Camden said.

"In this case, a little hint would be helpful," I said. "Let's go find Kenna."

CHAPTER THIRTEEN

"Forbidden Planet"

Kenna was a tall, attractive black woman dressed in the conservative uniform of the hotel staff: a gold skirt, white blouse, and burgundy jacket with a name tag in gold. She didn't mind answering my questions.

"You were in charge of the hospitality room on the third floor from six to ten Saturday night?"

"That's right."

"Can you remember who was in the room around eight, eight thirty?"

"That's going to be tough. All these people in costume, it's hard to tell, and I'm really not into science fiction, so I couldn't tell you who they were supposed to be."

"If you could describe the ones you remember?"

She thought for a moment. "There were some blue people with little white horns. There were people in tee shirts and lots of buttons and badges. There was a man with a really long knitted scarf. Some guy came in dressed sort of turn of the century style. He had on a really funny-looking wig, so he looked more like my grandmother. Then of course, there were many people in regular clothes."

"Do you recall a short round man in a Klingon costume?" I asked. "Those are the ones with ridged foreheads."

"Yeah, I'm familiar with Klingons," she said. "Was his headpiece crooked?"

"Yes. He had a bag with him. Did you notice if anyone went near it?"

She shook her head. "He probably put it near the door. Lots of people stack up their things while they eat. Nobody bothers their stuff. I have to say this about science fiction fans. They're usually polite and respectful of property. Don't get me started about some of the other groups we get in here."

"Anyone else come in? The Green Hornet, maybe?" At her confused frown, I clarified. "A masked man in a trench coat and fedora?"

"I don't remember anyone dressed like that. Superman came in, and Trillia."

"Trillia?" That was a new one for me and for Camden.

"Trillia Fernflower," Kenna explained. "The only reason I know that is because my sister had the entire series of Fernflower books. Each one's a different color and tells about a different fairy. Trillia's the purple one. There was a PBS special about the author last year. I remember she was really griping because she didn't like people dressing up like her characters. She said the real fairies didn't appreciate it." She grinned. "Now, we don't want to upset the little people, do we? Although this Trillia was a pretty big fairy."

This rang a fairy bell. "Did she have antenna?"

"Of course."

I thanked Kenna and Camden and I went in search of Antenna Woman. I hadn't realized before how many women were dressed like great big fairies.

"Here's your chance to prove yourself," I said. "Find this woman."

"The art room."

"That's more like it. I may keep you on."

He pointed to a large poster. "The Art of the Faerie" was written in swirly flowery letters. "Art Room, one to three."

***

A great many fairies, elves, dwarves, and assorted fantasy creatures crowded a section of the art room admiring the waterfalls,
sunlit woods, unicorns, and dragons prominently featured in "The
Art of the Faerie." Antenna Woman, in purple, was with a group
of similarly dressed women, gushing and cooing over the pictures.

"We'll wait till she's done," I said.

But Camden had halted, eyes wide. I wondered what had
caught his attention and then saw *Gallery of Fear*, all bloody flies
and chewed limbs. I had forgotten how revolting Leena Fay's
painting was and then recalled the young woman in the art room
had told me the death of Leena's sister had profoundly affected
her art. Camden didn't want to get any closer.

"Is it radiating black waves?" I asked.

"Good lord."

"Pretty sick, huh? Someone told me she used to do the fairy
stuff."

A cool voice behind me said, "I still do."

I turned to find myself eye to eye with a tall brunette. I recognized her from her picture. Unlike most of the convention-goers,
she was rail-thin and dressed in normal clothes, a smart-looking
gray business suit and pale pink blouse.

She offered a thin hand. "I'm Leena Fay."

I shook her hand. "David Randall. We were admiring your
painting."

"So I see."

I looked around for Camden, but he had disappeared. The
vibes were too bad, either way you looked at it. Despite the model
anorexia, Leena Fay was attractive. Her blue eyes checked me out
and apparently liked what they saw.

"You have to admit, compared to the fairies, this painting is a
little graphic," I said.

"Yes, but then, symbolism can be repugnant."

I pointed to a fly chewing on a bloody limb. Arm? Leg? I
couldn't tell. "What exactly is the symbolism here?"

"Have you ever experienced grief, Mr. Randall, a grief so profound and terrible that it feels as if your very soul were being eaten
alive?"

"Yes, I have."

She gave a small shrug. "Need I say more?"

"My condolences on the death of your sister."

A slight tremor went through her. "No doubt you've heard all the rumors. I don't wish to discuss it. It's an extremely painful topic."

"I understand." She was so sad. I went on hastily. "You feel that your artwork helps you cope?"

"Very much so."

A crowd of fairies saw her and came over, eager for auto-graphs, including one particularly large woman in a glittery crown who pushed forward to introduce herself as the Faerie Queen.

"Excuse me," Leena Fay said. As her excited fans surrounded her, I went looking for Camden. He was sitting out in the hallway, his head down on one hand. A lovely young woman in fairy robes bent over him, handing him a paper cup.

"You okay?" I asked.

"I needed to get away from that picture." He took a drink and smiled at the fairy. "Thanks."

She blushed. "Did anyone ever tell you you look like the good alien in *UFO Encounter*? You know, the one who stays on Earth and falls in love with Margery the waitress?"

"Many times," he said.

"Do you mind if I go get my friends? I'm sure they'd love to meet you."

"That's fine."

I watched her flit away. "We still need to talk to Antenna Woman."

The thought of returning to the art room made him shudder. "See if she'll come out here."

Leena Fay's admirers were still gathered in the art room, all talking excitedly about meeting their idol.

Antenna Woman was with the Faerie Queen. "Wasn't that re-markable?" she said to the Queen. "I can't believe we got to meet her."

"And she got to meet *me*," the Queen said. "I must go and tell my subjects."

As she made a grand exit, I asked Antenna Woman if I could ask her a few questions about Iris Hudson.

Antenna Woman stopped and gave me a long stare. "You're the man who was at Iris Hudson's last book signing."

"That's right. I'm investigating her murder. My name's David Randall."

Antenna Woman was impressed. "I'm Diana Davis, and the police have already talked to me, Mr. Randall. I'm in the clear."

"I'm sure you are. You told me you used to be friends with Ms. Hudson and how she reacted to criticism. I was hoping you might be able to tell me more."

"I'll do what I can," she said.

"While we were in line, a short Klingon came up to talk to me. He was carrying a bag full of stuff. Do you remember anything about that?"

She thought for a moment. "A short Klingon. No, I remember the cute blond man who was in front of me because he looked exactly like the elf-lord in *Timeless Treasure*."

"You can see him now," I said. "He's out in the hall."

Diana Davis was pleased by this and followed me out of the art room. Camden had attracted his own fan club by now. The fairy girl who'd brought him a drink was back with three more young women. All had apparently seen *Timeless Treasure*.

"See?" Diana said. "The resemblance is remarkable. The hair, the eyes, everything."

One of the fairy girls argued that he looked much more like King Melchior in *Over the Edge*.

"Yes, that's possible," Diana said, "but in that book, Mel Worthington is human."

"But his magic returns and he becomes king of Eldenfair because his mother was the Diamond Queen. The longer he stays, the more magical he becomes."

Diana got a little testy. "I know. You're not the only one who's read that series."

I had to put a stop to this right away or it would go on forever. "Camden," I said, "this is Diana Davis. You may remember her from Saturday."

He stood and shook her hand. "Yes, of course."

The fairy girls remembered they had to be somewhere and zipped off, giggling and waving good-by.

"Ms. Davis doesn't recall Stuart or any of his stuff," I said.

"Sorry," she said. "I really wasn't paying attention. I was hoping to reconnect with Iris. Sadly, there's no chance of that now."

"What about the man behind you?" I asked. "The one dressed as the Green Hornet who stormed off to tattle? Did you know him?"

"No, I didn't know him, and he hadn't said anything up until when she left."

"Would you recognize him if you saw him again?"

"I doubt it."

"Could you tell me more about the Dark Feud Ms. Hudson had with the fairy community?" I asked.

"Oh, you can read all about it on the Queen's blog, *Radiant Thoughts*," she said. "It's been going on for at least twenty years ever since we were all involved in a group we called the Seventh Elfin Realm, me and the Queen and Iris and a couple of other girls. We all loved the same fairy tale movies and TV shows, and we wrote stories and episodes with the characters or original stories. Whenever she had enough, the Queen would put them into a fanzine, but we haven't made one of those in several years now." She gave a sigh as if longing for those good old fairy days. "Iris wasn't a nice person, but I hate that she was stabbed like that. It kind of makes me nervous. Didn't the police catch the killer? Was it the short Klingon?"

"No, it's not the short Klingon," I said. "Stuart's a friend of ours. Somebody stole his knife and used it to kill Iris. Did you happen to notice him in the hospitality room around eight thirty the night of the cosplay contest?"

"I just stopped by for a moment to get a drink. I might have been there five minutes. Are you absolutely sure your friend is innocent?"

"We know Stuart," Camden said. "He'd never kill anyone."

"Well, it's unsettling to have a murder at the convention," Diana said. "It's reminding me of what happened to the artist Leena

Fay, There are so many rumors surrounding the death of her sister, and murder was one of them." She beamed at Camden. "Have you ever seen *Timeless Treasure*, Camden? You really do look like the elf-lord of the Silver Tree."

"No, I haven't," he said. "After today, I think I have to."

"Trust me, it's a compliment."

"Oh, well, thank you."

"You know, I think I have one of Leena's postcards with a picture from *Timeless Treasure*." She dug into her pocketbook. "It's from her Fairytale series, so you'll see it's quite different from her present artwork."

After a search, she pulled out a postcard with a glossy finish which she showed to both of us. The art work was indeed quite different. The Silver Tree was an elaborate swirl of twisty branches decorated with little silver lights. The background was a deep blue sprinkled with stars and a silver crescent moon set above the tree.

"That's beautiful," Camden said.

"Yes, it's really a shame she stopped painting lovely scenes like this." Diana put the postcard back in her pocketbook and checked her watch. "I'd love to stay and chat some more, but I'm meeting some fairy friends for a panel on Fairy Lore of Ireland. Nice to have met both of you."

She went down the hall.

"I'm glad you're good for something, o mighty elf-lord," I said. "The fairies wouldn't have been so friendly if I hadn't known one of their own kind. Get anything from the handshake?"

"Only what she told us." He took a deep breath as if shaking off the last effects of *Gallery of Fear*. "That Silver Tree picture was certainly the opposite of what she paints now."

"Would you say *Gallery of Fear* is her way of coping with loss, an expression of grief?"

Camden shook his head. "That painting's not about grief."

"Okay, so there's maybe a little anger mixed in."

"Revenge. Hatred. Death. It almost knocked me off my feet."

"Then you probably don't want to shake Miss Fay's hand."

"No, thank you."

"I want to ask her a few more questions," I said. "Where will you be?"

"As far away as possible. The UFO exhibit."

I went back into the art room. Leena Fay stood talking with two earnest-looking men in medieval costumes.

"The colors are so powerful," one man was saying. "I can't help but be reminded of Lubovitch's early spacescapes."

"Do you think you'll ever go back to the lovely rainbow series?" the other man asked.

Leena Fay shook her head. "I can't see that happening."

"We certainly respect your artistic decisions."

She thanked them, and they left. She saw me and gave me a curious look.

"A few more questions, if you don't mind," I said.

She motioned to *Gallery of Fear*. "I think I've said all I can say."

"Not questions about your artwork. Did you know Iris Hudson?"

She slowly repeated the name. "Iris Hudson. I've heard that name before. Wasn't there something about her being murdered? She was an author, I believe."

"She wrote the *Dark Star* series."

"I'm sorry. I don't read much science fiction these days. There was a time when I was deeply into science fiction and fantasy, but that, too, is past."

"I'm investigating her murder."

Leena Fay grimaced. "How dreadful. Do you do this kind of thing often?"

"Every now and then."

"No wonder you related to my painting."

Recoiled, maybe.

"Have you lost a sister, as well. Mr. Randall?"

"My daughter." I didn't add that I knew exactly where she was and often spoke with her. Leena Fay did not have the same comfort.

"Then you do understand how profoundly one's life can change."

"Yes." Having Lindsey appear in my dreams and help me solve mysteries was not something I could have ever predicted.

"I wish I could help you, but I didn't know Iris Hudson." Her gaze went beyond me to another group of fans standing by another dark painting who indicated they wanted a photo of her. She looked back at me. "Your conversation has touched my soul, Mr. Randall. Not everyone is as empathetic, always clamoring for the flowers and rainbows I used to paint."

"I don't like to listen to rumors, Ms Fay. Would you tell me what happened to your sister?"

"Cancer," she said. "She was only forty-eight."

"I'm very sorry."

"Perhaps we can talk again, but I should speak to my fans. If you would excuse me, please."

Twice she had denied knowing Iris Hudson, but if at one time she had been, as she said, deeply into science fiction and fantasy, she would have come across the *Dark Star* series. But right now it seemed nothing mattered to Leena Fay was finding solace in her ghastly art.

CHAPTER FOURTEEN

"The Flying Saucer"

At the UFO Believer booth, Camden was looking through a box of *Sky Watcher* magazines. He'd already chosen three and set them aside. He doesn't say much about it, but I knew he suspected he might have been the result of an alien romance between his birth mother and this mysterious unknown father I liked to call Space Dad. It was the psychic thing. He wanted to know how he got it and why. The UFO explanation made as much sense as anything else.

"Completing your set?" I asked.

"Almost." He held up a book titled *Mystery From the Heavens*. "How much is this?" he asked the woman behind the table. Against all odds, she was dressed as a normal person, SuperCon tee shirt and jeans, her brown hair in an untidy braid, her bangs in her eyes.

"Six fifty."

"Can't your super secret powers tell how much it is?" I asked.

"I'm lucky to be breathing after seeing that picture."

The woman looked interested. "What picture's that?"

"A little number called *Gallery of Fear* by Leena Fay," I said.

"Oh, yeah, she's a legend. I've got one of her rainbow series, signed and everything. Is she here? I'd heard she was going to make an appearance. She's been in seclusion since her sister's death."

Camden handed her the book and three magazines. "I'll take

these."

The woman took Camden's money and gave him his change. "There you go."

He saw something else on the table he liked. "How much is this copy of *Steller*?"

"Fourteen fifty."

He leafed through the book. "I don't think I have this one."

"It's a number four. Not too rare. It's number three that's hard to find."

"I have two copies of number three at home."

The woman got excited. "Are you kidding? Would you sell one? I'll give you fifty dollars for it, plus that book. I've been looking for a number three forever."

"Okay," he said. "I'll bring it by later."

We moved on and found a relatively quiet corner of the room so I could check in with my clients. Geoff reported that he had checked out of the Hilton.

"The police said I could leave the Hilton but to stay in Parkland. I'm staying with some friends at 1266 Baker Avenue."

I thanked him for the update.

"I've looked through as many of our past posts as I could and found nothing that could be considered threatening, but I'll continue the search," he said. "At least it gives me something to do."

Pastor Gary, unfortunately, was in, and not happy with my daily report. I held the phone away from my ear so Camden could hear Ingram's sputtering.

"I expect results, Mr. Randall, reasonable, useful results! What am I paying you for, anyway?"

I brought the phone back to reply. "If you want the Angel of Truth really and completely stopped, it may take more time than you like."

"I will not pay a penny more until you bring me concrete evidence Eric O'Conner has something to do with this. I am going to confront this man and let him know he cannot defile a servant of the Lord!"

"Yes, sir," I said and ended the call. "Always a pleasure talking to the reverend."

"I'll be glad when you're through with him," Camden said.

"If I hadn't promised Kary I'd help her father, I'd forget about finding the Angel of Truth," I said.

***

We got home by four, in time for me to have Kary's Diet Coke ready when she came in from school. After thanking me, she sat down in the island and placed her book bag beside her chair. "The next time you and Cam go to the convention, I'm coming with you."

I settled in the blue armchair. "We're going back after supper. Camden's made a deal with one of the booksellers."

"That works for me. Did you find out anything today?"

"Not much. But we've got a handle on when the knife must have been taken."

"How was it taken?" she asked.

"There are a couple of possibilities. Stuart says someone bumped into him on that same floor at the elevator, and he put his bag down in the hospitality room. The hotel worker on duty remembers seeing him there, but says bags were stacked everywhere."

"So you've talked to everyone who might have seen Stuart that day?"

"All his fellow Klingons, Druids and Vulcans and Borgs."

"Oh, my," she said with a grin.

"The hotel staff, the convention folks, and even the woman who was in line with him and Camden to get a book signed before Hudson stormed off. I should also talk to everyone who was in the food court and the art room Saturday afternoon. It's like looking for a needle in a haystack. No, I should say a speck of dust in an asteroid belt."

She took a sip of her cola. "Maybe I can help with that."

"It's worth a try. I certainly won't mind having you along."

"I should have enough time to check these papers before supper, then."

"More papers?"

"This is the last of them."

"I'll be glad to help."

We decided to use the dining room table. Camden was in the kitchen, grating cheese into a long baking dish. There was lasagna in our future.

Kary pulled a stack of papers from her bag and gave me half. "All you have to do is check their spelling. I have some stickers for them." She rooted in the bag and brought out pages of brightly colored grape and strawberry smelling stickers. "Be sure you put one on each paper."

"Even if they can't spell?"

"The purple ones say, 'Good Try.'"

The cartoon grapes had encouraging smiles. "So they do."

Bobby Farrington had written about a terrible "strom" that had "leaved" everything "tor up." Bobby got a purple sticker. Jenna Tilson-Barr, however, got the coveted strawberry sticker that said "Way To Go!" I had a feeling Jenna Tilson-Barr got whatever she wanted.

"How about Angel Martinez?" I asked. I turned the paper so she could see it. "Looks like a good story with lots of Spanish words mixed in."

"Strawberry for sure. Angel's working really hard on his English." She paused in her work. "Did you happen to see an angel statue in the Story Garden?"

I placed a strawberry sticker on Angel's paper. "I saw quite a few."

"This one would be by herself, looking down with a peaceful expression, hands clasped."

"I think I remember one like that. What about it?"

She sat back in her chair. "I hadn't thought of her in a long time. Years ago, I guess I was seven or eight, we didn't have the mega-church, but a small congregation, and that angel statue stood in the cemetery. I don't know whose grave she was protecting. The words had worn off the gravestone. But as a child I always thought she was the angel Gabriel, the one who told Mary she was going to have a baby. I thought when I was old enough to have a baby, that same angel would come to me." She gave a slight laugh. "That didn't work out, did it?"

I wasn't sure what to say. Kary so rarely talked about her early life in the church.

She straightened and picked up the next paper. "I'm not sure what made me think of her except all this business with my father is bringing back memories. Not all of them bad, I guess. I do remember him insisting the angel be moved to the new church. I don't know why when he could afford all those new statues." She fixed me with a direct dark gaze. "You asked if I had a favorite hymn. This is going to sound odd, but I like an old one called 'Nothing But the Blood.' Sounds weird, I know, but it's the only one I ever remember hearing my mother sing. She never got to sing very much because my father always had these special soloists and groups, especially once he got on TV."

"Sounds a little dark."

She chuckled. "Gotta be dark and scary to keep that money rolling in."

Camden came to the table, carrying a glass of iced tea. "Supper will be ready in about thirty minutes. Anybody want anything to drink?"

"I still have plenty of Coke, thanks," Kary said.

"Randall?"

"I'm fine. Have a sticker."

"I'll take a grape." He put the sticker on the back of his hand and then put his hand on Kary's shoulder. "You okay?"

"Just taking a stroll down memory lane," she said. "Cam, what's your favorite hymn?"

He thought a moment. "There are several, but I think I'll go with 'His Eye is on the Sparrow.' How 'bout you, Randall?"

I stacked my papers neatly and handed them to Kary. "'We Will Rock You.'"

This made her laugh. "David."

"Isn't that a version of 'Rock of Ages'?"

"I dare you to sing that."

"Kary, no," Camden said. "The vibrations will ruin the lasagna."

"I'll take that chance," I said, and launched into song.

***

After several choruses of my favorite hymn and large helpings of lasagna, the three of us went to the convention. Kary and I wandered through the dealers' room. Kary had worn jeans and a pale blue sweater and had her silky blonde hair in a ponytail—a subdued outfit for ExtravaganzaCon, but this didn't keep dazzled fans from approaching with various tributes.

"Hail, Galadriel the Fair!"

"Aphrodite! How are things on Mount Olympus?"

Kary treated all this with the same serene patience she used on the second graders of Lakeside Elementary. "From the way everyone's acting, you'd never guess that two people have been murdered in this hotel," she said to me.

"I know. Bizarre, isn't it? But we are dealing in fantasy here."

She looked around the huge room swarming with costumed fans and busy dealers. "I see what you mean about finding possible witnesses."

We met Camden at the UFO booth where he'd sold his book to the very happy seller and was now fifty dollars richer.

"Drinks are on you," I said.

He folded the money in his jeans pocket. "I think I'll put this in the baby fund. What's next?"

"I'm not sure Kary has been admired enough, so we're going to continue our tour of the dealers' room." The sight of a familiar large square shape towering over the booths in the neighboring aisle made me revise this plan. "Or we could talk to Jordan. I need to ask him about O'Conner."

Jordan greeted us and told me he didn't have anything on O'Conner. "You realize we're working our way through a few hundred people" He fixed me with a gaze from his sharp little blue eyes. "Why the interest in O'Conner, Randall? Do you know something I don't know? Something I should know?"

"He was on the eighth floor the night Iris was murdered."

"So were a lot of people. What makes you suspect he had anything to do with the murder?"

It was unlikely O'Conner would have had an opportunity to get Stuart's knife, murder Iris, and then upset the cosplay contest. "Just following a hunch," I said. "Have you narrowed down the time of Iris Hudson's death?"

"That's still under investigation, but the chances of narrowing it further than between eight and ten are slim. Do you know anything more about Sean Synder's death?" He swung his gaze to Camden to include him in the question.

Camden shook his head. "No, sorry."

"Then I suggest both of you let the police handle all this." He gave Kary a nod. "Evening, Kary," he said, and strolled off.

Jordan's usual warning. But this time, I didn't have much of a comeback.

CHAPTER FIFTEEN

"A Fairy Tale"

Before Stuart left for work Tuesday morning, I asked if the Druid he'd seen in the elevator with the Vulcans and Borgs was wearing a white robe.

"I don't think so," Stuart said. "Seems like it was gray."

"Did you see his face? What did he look like?"

"He had his hood over his face. You know druids are shy."

And possibly murderous. "Did you see him in the hospitality room?"

"I don't remember. Sorry."

"Can you at least remember how tall he was? Was he fat? Thin?"

"Just tall."

So I was on the lookout for a druid in gray who was "just tall."

I'd managed to miss Kary, so instead of enjoying her lovely radiance at the breakfast table, I was stuck with Ellin. I almost wished Ellin would go back on the caffeine. I didn't think it was possible for her to be any crankier. She crammed things into her attaché case, glaring at Camden as he carried his Pop-Tarts to the kitchen counter.

"You're going back to the convention? You've been there for days."

"I'm trying to help Randall," he said.

"You know I hate it when you help Randall. You always damage yourself while he gets barely a scratch."

"I haven't damaged myself this time."

She gave him a look and pointed at his forehead where the star-shaped bruise was still visible.

"But, Ellie, we have to find Iris Hudson's killer and Sean Snyder's killer, too. Why don't you come to the convention with me?"

"I have a network to run."

He sat down on one of the stools at the counter. "You could stop by for a little while, couldn't you?"

"I have an idea," she said.

Ellin's ideas involve pain, suffering, and pay back. "Hold on to your Pop-Tarts," I said.

"I hate to think of you turning to the Enforcettes for comfort and protection all the time. Let me make sure everything is running smoothly at the studio, and I'll meet you at the convention in about an hour."

"That sounds great," Camden said. "We'll see you then."

She gave him a kiss and hurried out.

"Well, how about that?" he said.

"Did you use a Vulcan mind-meld on your wife?"

"Just my natural charm."

"Don't kid yourself. She's got something else planned." I took out my phone. "Before we head over to the con, I need to look up *Radiant Thoughts*, the Faerie Queen's blog."

"Do you need a radiant thought?"

"I need to see if her blog sheds any light on the Dark Feud the fairies had with Iris."

The Queen's full name was Queen Jewel Moonlight of the Seventh Elfin Realm. Her real name was Jodi Anderson, and her thoughts were anything but radiant. The current ones were nice little journal entries about her experiences at ExtravaganzaCon, but a search of the Archives for Dark Feud unearthed a deluge of faerie fury that started twenty years ago.

"Camden, listen to this. 'My loyal subjects and all who hold dear our precious Seventh Elfin Realm, it is with a heavy heart that I report Iris Hudson continues to support her ridiculous and unfounded theory that, as a genre, fantasy is substandard to science fiction. As you know, my loyal subjects, Iris Hudson was once a treasured part of our family, known to us as Elphinia Day Star, but she has renounced that name and profaned it by bestowing it upon the lead character of her *Dark Star* novels.'"

"How dare she?" Camden said.

"How dare she, indeed. But wait, there's more. 'Not only that, my dear subjects, she has stolen ideas from *Wildflower Wonders, Jewels of the Nine Kingdoms*, and *Tales of the Seventh Elfin Realm*, lied when confronted with proof, and to this day refuses to apologize for all the pain and heartache her plagiarism has caused. By my royal order, I declare that she be expelled from the Seventh Elfin Realm, shunned by all who once called her friend, and never spoken of again.' Then she goes on to speak of her again in un-fairy-like terms. I won't sear your little elf ears by reading them aloud."

"I've never heard of *Wildflower Wonders* or those other books."

"Hang on." I searched the blog for the three titles the Queen had mentioned. "Oh, those are some of the Queen's fanzines from a few decades ago." I set my phone down. "It might be helpful to read through a couple of those and see what caused all the fuss. If Iris really plagiarized someone, they might have gotten annoyed."

***

True to her word, Ellin met us at the convention. We showed her around the dealers' room, starting with the jewelry. Ellin was impressed in spite of herself. She was pleased by the selection of celestial earrings and spent a long time deciding which ones to buy.

"Teresa asked me to buy her some of Nebula Studio's prints," she said. "Where would they be?"

"Probably in the art room," Camden said.

I was ready for this. "Let's show Ellin our favorite picture."

"You can show Ellie our favorite picture. I'll wait in the hall."

Ellin finished her jewelry shopping, I bought some star earrings for Kary, and we went to the art room. I expected her to be repulsed by *Gallery of Fear*, but she stared at it thoughtfully.

"I've seen something like this before."

"In a nightmare, probably," I said.

"It wasn't this particular painting, but a similar one called *Night-mare Garden*. It was a collection of pictures, all like this, by this same artist, Leena Fay."

I often forgot that in her quest to have a variety of stories on the PSN, Ellin came in contact with all types of creative people. True, most of them were delusional, but she could be a good source of information if she was in the loop. However, she was rarely around when I was discussing a case with Camden and Kary. I often forgot that, too.

"Leena told me her sister died of cancer. Do you know anything more about this?"

Oddly enough, Ellin did. "I did my usual background research before the program. Leena suffered for years from depression. She was coming to terms with it when her sister died. Her sister had recently gotten out of an abusive relationship and was starting a new life when she was diagnosed. This almost killed Leena, too, but painting was her way of dealing with grief."

"Do you know her sister's name?"

"I believe it was Nancy. Something with an 'N.' I could look it up for you."

An abusive relationship. A name beginning with "N." "Natalie, maybe?"

"Yes, that's it."

There's no way you could've known about Natalie.

That's what Sean Snyder said when Camden revealed his dark secret.

We went out to the hallway where Camden waited a safe distance from the painting. "Camden, Sean Snyder's wife was Natalie, right? I may have a connection. I need to know if Natalie had a sister named Leena."

I took out my phone and looked up the obituary for Natalie Snyder. Her maiden name was Montgomery, and according to her obituary she was survived by her husband, Sean, and her sister, Nora Montgomery.

But no mention of a Leena Fay.

I put my phone away and looked around at the costumed crowd. There were lots of cloaks, all colors, especially gray. The

Enforcettes had formed a comfy circle around Camden, a circle that included Ellin, looking every inch an Enforcette herself.

Tiger caught sight of me and gestured. "David, come here. We've come up with a great idea. At one-thirty today, we're supposed to take part in a panel discussion about warrior women in science fiction. O'Conner's bound to be there to make trouble. If you and Cam are there, you can catch him."

"It's worth a try."

"Dawn should have had him."

"Don't start that again," Dawn said.

"Let's do it!" Brianna said. "The panel's in the Mercury Room."

Ellin didn't say anything negative about the Enforcettes, probably because they had been brimming with battle plans instead of hanging all over Camden. He was explaining the group's problem with O'Conner to her when I saw Geoff Snyder walking slowly down the hallway. He looked older and grayer with no trace of his smirking smile.

When I asked him about Nora Montgomery, he said, "Sean didn't want any contact with Natalie's family, and there wasn't any reason for me to associate with them. It was my understanding the sisters were estranged. What does this have to do with Sean's murder?"

"I'm trying to find out," I said. "Did you know Sean was abusing his wife?"

Geoff's face went red. "He did not abuse her!" Several people turned to stare, and he lowered his voice, still angry. "He may have hit her once or twice, but he was sorry. It wasn't like he beat her. A slap, maybe. You know how you lose control."

"No, Geoff, I don't lose control like that, but apparently you do, and Sean must have, too. If you knew that was going on and didn't stop it, you're just as guilty as Sean."

He looked shocked. "It was none of my business."

"And look where it got you."

He started to say something else, then paused. He blinked several times, as if holding back tears. "Yes, look where it got me. Standing in the middle of some idiotic space toy store, my brother dead, my career uncertain, arguing with a small-time detective and a psychic, neither of whom can tell me who murdered Sean."

"I'll find out who did this," I said.

He gave a short laugh that was almost a sob. "I don't have anyone else to turn to, do I?"

CHAPTER SIXTEEN

"The Man from Planet X"

While Camden showed Ellin exhibits she might be interested in for the PSN, I went in search of fairy fanzines. There were dozens of them, but eventually I found a few vintage copies of *Wildflower Wonders*, *Jewels of the Nine Kingdoms*, and *Tales of the Seventh Elfin Realm*. The fairy in charge of the booth had apparently taken a bath in glitter, but fortunately *Wildflower Wonders* and the other zines were protected by clear plastic wrappers. Most of the stories had been written by the Queen Jewel Moonlight, but two stories in the zine, 'Dark Fantasy' and 'Unending Starlight,' were by Natalie Montgomery and illustrated by Nora Montgomery. The copyright on *Wildflower Wonders* was twenty years ago.

Glitter Girl didn't mind if I stood to one side and read. Natalie's stories were beautifully written, and her sister's illustrations intricate and fanciful. In fact, I recognized one of the trees with its twisty branches and little silver lights. I thanked Glitter Girl and bought *Wildflower Wonders*.

"Good choice," she said. "That's one of the best zines."

"Looks like it was written before the Dark Feud," I said.

Up went her pink glittered eyebrows. "Oh, you know about that? Yeah, it was published right before Iris Hudson was kicked out. That was, let me see, not long after that issue of *Wildflower*

Wonders was published, so, maybe twenty years ago. Did you know Iris was killed the other night right here in this hotel? Bad luck for her, huh?"

I wouldn't exactly call it luck. "Are you a member of the Seventh Elfin Realm?" I asked.

"No, I'm in the Rainbow Realm."

That explained the multicolored sparkles. "Do you have anything else by Natalie Montgomery?"

"Just *Wildflower Wonders*. Her stuff's lovely, isn't it? I wish she'd written more, but she only wrote about ten stories, then just faded away. I think she was planning to write a series and go pro, you know, professional? That's what I hope to do some day."

Two customers came up, both dressed as elves, and Glitter Girl turned her attention to them.

I managed to get the top layer of glitter off my hands and found Camden and Ellin at a UFO booth, chatting with a fellow dressed as a Reticulated Gray, all bulb-like head and dark blank eyes. The alien and Ellin were getting along, so I showed Camden Natalie Montgomery's stories in *Wildflower Wonders* and Nora Montgomery's artwork.

"Recognize this particular tree?"

"I believe that would be an Early Leena Fay."

"I believe you would be right," I said. "I haven't read the whole *Dark Star* series, so I'm not as familiar with Hudson's style, but would you be able to tell if Iris used any of Natalie's work?"

"I think so," he said.

We took a lunch break and at one-thirty, went to the Mercury Room for the panel on warrior women. The Enforcettes were joined by experts on other fierce, independent science fiction and fantasy women characters.

"You should enjoy this," I said to Ellin. "These are your people, ball-bustin' women of the universe."

"Keep talking like that," she said, "and you'll see some ball busting."

She took a seat down front while Camden and I patrolled the edges of the room. Toward the back, I saw Thomas Warburn, Captain Clark of *Beyond the Asteroids*, and made my way over to him.

The Captain had been something of a ladies' man. So was this guy.

"Great gals, those Enforcettes," he said. "Wonderful costumes. I appreciate their attention to detail."

"Yeah, as close to the real thing as you can get."

He chuckled. "Sure makes a hell of a lot more interesting panel. I tell you, I've been on some dull ones. Thought the one the other night would never end."

"Which one was that?"

"Authors' Roundtable. You don't want to get some of those windbags started on their work and its lasting influence, that's for sure."

"Is that the panel Iris Hudson was supposed to attend?"

"I'm glad she didn't. I don't want to speak ill of the dead, but that was one nasty woman."

"You said some nice things at her memorial service," I said.

"Yes, well, that was another performance. Wouldn't look good for Captain Clark to bad-mouth a famous author, now would it?"

"You said you had the pleasure of working with her. Did Iris have a connection to *Beyond the Asteroids?*"

"Oh, back in the early days, she used to write for us. Must be twenty years ago. Can't really say that was a pleasure, though."

This was news. "Iris Hudson wrote for *Beyond the Asteroids?*"

He chuckled. "Oh, she never claimed us. Once she got into her serious work, TV was beneath her. You remember 'The Vats of Orion'? That's hers, and so is 'Battle for Neptune.'"

Two of the worst episodes. "I don't remember seeing her name in the credits."

"She used the name Terrance Fitzner. Not many people know that. I guess it'll come out now. Lord, she was an unhappy woman! Here she is, working for a top TV drama, a landmark science fiction series, and all she does is bitch and complain. I don't know how Vincent worked with her."

"If she was so awful, how did they become partners in the first place?" I asked.

"Beats me."

"Wasn't Parnell being a little presumptuous, taking Iris's place in the Authors' Roundtable?"

"Oh, he definitely deserved to be there, if only for putting up with Iris Hudson all these years."

"Is he an author?"

"Yeah, he had a couple of things published when *Asteroids* was first out. Never read 'em myself, but I think his books were well-received."

This was getting complicated. "He wasn't interested in writing for your show?"

The captain shrugged. "Not everybody can write a TV script. Now the *Dark Star* books are ten times better than the episodes Hudson wrote for us. I know authors improve over the years, but she *really* improved."

I wondered if Parnell was the power behind the throne, and Iris the Evil Queen. Did he write the *Beyond the Asteroids* scripts? Did he write the *Dark Star* books? Did Iris Hudson have something on him, something so horrible he allowed her to take all the credit? If she wasn't blackmailing him, why put up with her? Why not get rid of her?

Which is what Parnell might have decided to do.

Camden came over. "Randall, I've spotted O'Conner. The guy in the Batman costume."

"Captain, thanks for your time," I said. "Camden, tell the girls I've got him."

I casually made my way around the room until I was close to Batman. He had on the trademark mask, but the mask didn't cover his chin. I'd seen that chin before, poking out from another mask. It was indeed the infamous Green Hornet.

Before he could react, I took hold of his arm and propelled him out into the hall. "I need to talk to you."

He tried to get away, but even though he was almost my height, he was a scrawny Batman, and I had a firm grip. "Who the hell are you?"

I removed his mask with a swift tug. "You don't know me, but I believe you've run into my friend, the Star Prince?"

I yanked him around the corner and into an empty suite. The cleaning service must have just finished. I shut and locked the door.

O'Conner's chin was his best feature. The rest of his face was doughy and nondescript. He scowled and tried to play macho man. "You can't do this! I'm calling the front desk! I'll tell the con organizers."

"Good. I hear they're looking for you. To tell you you're banned from any of their cons for life. While you're doing that, I'll call the police. There's a little matter of a stolen trophy."

Eric O'Conner realized his Batmobile was about to go over a cliff and crumpled like a dead spider. "I'm sorry! I'm sorry! I didn't realize your friend was so light! It was centrifugal force, man. I didn't mean it."

"Shut up. I might save you from the wrath of the Enforcettes, but you're going to have to answer some questions." I showed him my ID. "My name is David Randall, and I'm investigating the murder of Iris Hudson. Where were you at eight PM Saturday night?"

"I didn't kill her! Are you crazy? I wasn't even in the hotel!"

"Oh, yes, you were. You were in the hall on the eighth floor around eight o'clock."

His eyes bugged out. "How did you know that?"

"You were in a hurry to see the Enforcettes' skit and bumped into some folks, including a short Klingon. He remembers your outfit. Come on, Eric. What were you doing there?"

"I didn't murder anybody!"

"Okay, I'm calling the cops. You'll talk to them."

"Hey! I didn't do anything!" he said. "I didn't have anything against Iris Hudson."

"You weren't very happy at her book signing. Do the police know that?"

I was finally getting through all the panic. "Okay, okay, look. I'll tell you what I know. I'm harmless. I ruin things, I don't kill them."

"What's the deal with that?"

"It's fun."

"Do you have something approaching a real life?"

"Don't give me that. You mundanes think we're all crazy."

"No, I just think *you're* crazy. You're talking to a fan, buddy, from *Forbidden Planet* to MST3K. I'm not putting down your obsession. I'm trying to keep you alive."

He sat down on the bed, his expression sulky. "Like I said, it's fun, okay? Cheryl thinks she's so tough."

"Cheryl?"

"Brianna' real name. Everyone's supposed to call her Brianna now. I mean, she's really into the Enforcettes. Too into it, if you ask me."

"I didn't. So why were you on the eighth floor? I know you're not staying in the hotel."

"Okay, okay, let me think."

I folded my arms and leaned against the door in case Eric O'Conner got any wild ideas about rushing me and escaping.

He wanted to pout. "I was playing a game on the ninth floor, and I lost track of the time. I was in a hurry to get to the cosplay contest. I was taking stairs instead of waiting for the elevator, but there were people standing on the landing, blocking the way so I changed my mind and ran to the elevator."

"Who where these people?"

"Two people. I only caught a glimpse of them. They were arguing. Fan stuff. You know, in episode six, Commander Cheeseball was wearing a red tunic. No, it was yellow. That kind of thing."

"What were they saying, exactly?"

O'Conner groaned as if I were applying thumbscrews. "I don't know. Sheesh. Something about *Dark Star*. Fans are always arguing about those books. Yeah, one of them said something about Wildhaven and that's always in the *Dark Star* books."

"Two women?"

"Two big fat women."

"Was one of them dressed like a purple fairy?"

"I don't remember what they were wearing. I saw them and took off."

Someone pounded on the door. O'Conner jumped behind the bed. "Randall," Tiger's voice said, "have you got O'Conner in there?"

O'Conner dropped and scrambled under the bed. I opened the door. "Sorry, girls. He got away. Try the lobby."

"Damn." They went down the hall.

I shut the door. "You owe me."

He spoke from under the bed. "Whatever you want."

"For starters, from now on, you're going to leave the Enforcettes alone. No more crashing their skits. Find someone else to annoy. Second, if you remember anything, any detail, no matter how small, about the night Iris Hudson was killed, you are to contact me."

"Okay, okay."

"I don't believe you're sincere, Eric. Let me get Tiger back in here."

"Okay! I said okay." He slowly crawled out from under the bed. "Can I go?"

"No. You were in line with my friend and a few other people to get your book signed by Iris Hudson. Not only were you annoyed by her leaving early, you saw the knife when Stuart showed it to me and Camden. Convince me you didn't steal that knife and kill her."

O'Conner went white. "You don't honestly believe that!"

"You've got motive and opportunity."

"I didn't see any knife! I was waiting to get my book signed."

"You don't remember a Klingon coming up with a bag of junk?"

He stared at me. "Do you know how many people are dressed like Klingons at this con? No, I wasn't paying any attention to that."

"You were very angry when Hudson left," I said.

"Yes, and I did something about it. You can ask the con organizers! I went right to them and told them about Hudson. They apologized and gave me a free pass to all the evening activities. That meant I didn't have to pay extra to get in to the cosplay contest, and my main reason for being here was to get to that contest and screw with the Enforcettes. You know for a fact I was there. Can I go now?"

"No. What have you got against Pastor Ingram, Angel of Truth?"

I hoped the stress of the situation would make it impossible for him to lie, and I was right.

His face turned red. "That sanctimonious old fart! He deserves every bad thing anyone ever said about him!"

"What did he do to you besides fire you from the church?"

"Fire me? He didn't fire me. I got out of there. Do you know what he said about science fiction and fantasy and people who like that kind of stuff? He said it was evil and perverted because only God knows the future!"

"A lot of people don't like science fiction and fantasy."

"Yeah, but to say it was the devil putting all those crazy ideas into their heads? He's the one who's mental. He's exactly like Darth Vader, only worse."

"Worse than Darth Vader is pretty bad. What do you mean?" I asked.

O'Conner had run out of steam. He sat down on the bed. His shoulders sagged. "You know. Luke Skywalker has to go through a movie and a half plus lose a hand to find out the main villain of the whole saga is his father. I had to wait twenty-five years and accidentally find a note from my mother."

Ah. His reference to "sins of the fathers' in one of his videos came back to me. "You believe Gary Ingram is your father?"

"Yeah," he said. "What a surprise, huh?"

Good God, I thought. Could this guy be Kary's half-brother? "That's something you'd better know for sure."

He looked at his Batman mask and shook his head. "Look, I had nothing to do with anybody's murder, but I'll admit I'm the Angel of Truth. Freedom of speech, man. I can put whatever I want on the Internet. How did you find out about that?"

"He hired me to find you."

"Of course he did. My mom struggled to bring me up. She could have used the help—but he just blew her off."

"Do you have proof you're his son?" I asked.

"My mom worked at the church when he was first starting out. Gillian Wilson. She died last year, and I found a note in her Bible asking me to forgive her, telling me she'd had an affair with someone in the church. There was a letter from Gary Ingram threatening her if she ever said anything. I can put two and two together." His voice shook with emotion and then he got control. "I had to do something, and I've got plenty of makeup and wigs for my con costumes, so I made some videos.

"Why didn't you confront him directly?"

"Oh, I tried to tell him I needed to talk with him, but it was impossible. He was always too busy, or preparing a sermon, or in a meeting with his rich friends. He never heard a word a peon like me said. So I thought, 'Okay, buddy, here's something that will make you pay attention.'"

"You definitely got his attention."

"I got the job because I wanted to see what he was like—give him a chance. But I found out he disowned his real daughter because she got pregnant. Yet he swept it under the rug that he got my mother pregnant when he had just married his wife. He's the biggest hypocrite on the face of the earth."

Irony at its finest. "Yeah, I know about the daughter. So what has to happen to satisfy you? Does Ingram need to go on TV and declare that you're the rightful heir to the throne?"

O' Conner took a long moment as if deciding what he wanted. "He doesn't have to do it on TV. But the world needs to know what he is. Tell him he has to admit I exist or I'll blast my story all over the Internet."

In that moment, he looked young and sad, another child discarded by the Great and Powerful Pastor Ingram. "Everything you do is for attention, right?" I said.

There was a reluctant grin. "Yeah, pretty much." His grin faded.

"Yes," I said. "And we're going to talk about that. But there's something you have to do first."

I went out into the hall and flagged down Brianna. "In here." She came in and I shut the door. "I'll referee."

O'Conner stood up, but Brianna didn't attack. She stared at him, arms folded. "You bastard," she said. "Where's our trophy?"

"Is that all you want, that cheap hunk of plastic?"

"Yes, that's all I want. I suppose you think you're so smart, ruining our skits like that. When are you going to grow up?"

"Grow up? Look at you in that—that whatever you call that outfit!"

I cleared my throat. "I don't think you have a case, Batman."

They glared at each other for a few minutes. Then Brianna said, "All we want is our trophy."

"It's in the trunk of my car."

"I want you to give it back, leave the convention, and keep away from me."

O'Conner started to say something else, looked at me, and changed his mind. "All right."

I accompanied Brianna and O'Conner as we went out to his car, a beat up Camry in sad need of a paint job. He unlocked the trunk, and handed her the shooting star trophy.

"Here," he said. "I'm sorry."

She stared. "You're sorry?"

"Yes. I'm sorry. It won't happen again."

"Oh," she said. "Well, okay, then." She tucked the trophy under her arm. "Thanks, David."

"My pleasure."

O'Conner watched her walk back into the convention hall. Then he looked at me. "So are you going to talk to Gary Ingram?"

"Do you really want a man like that to say he's your father?" His daughter gets along just fine without him, I wanted to say. "Or do you just want money?"

"No!" he said. "I worked at that church. I know where all that money comes from. People who can't afford it. People he scares into believing they're going to hell. I don't want any of it. I—I guess I don't know what I want."

My estimation of Eric O'Conner went up several more points. "I'll talk to him," I said. "Do you still have your mother's note and the threatening letter from Ingram? I'd like to see them."

"Yeah," he said. "I still have them."

"I'll follow you home."

When O'Conner parked in the driveway of 456 Edgewood, I pulled in behind and waited while he went into his house. He returned a few minutes later and handed me two well-worn pieces of paper.

"I'd like to borrow these," I said.

"Yeah, if you think it'll do any good."

I gave him one of my cards. "Here's how to get in touch with me."

He took the card and offered his hand for me to shake. "Thanks, man. Sorry for all the, you know."

"You're welcome," I said, but all I could think of was, I'd better find out the truth before I say anything to Kary about this.

CHAPTER SEVENTEEN

"Labyrinth"

When I returned to the Mercury Room, the warrior women panel was over. I found Thomas Warburn chatting with Ellin. The Captain was turning on the charm.

"This is remarkably refreshing," he said. "I've never met anyone who's never seen *Beyond the Asteroids.*"

"My husband's the fan, not me," Ellin said. "When I was growing up, I had to watch what my older sisters liked. Their tastes ran to sitcoms and MTV."

"So all this must seem very silly to you."

"Actually, it's entertaining. I enjoyed this panel discussion. I've enjoyed talking with you."

He gave a little bow. "It's been my pleasure."

Ellin handed him one of her cards. "I'm the producer for the Psychic Service Network. I'd like to have you as a guest on one of our programs some time, to talk about what it was like working with psychic characters during the filming of *Beyond the Asteroids.*"

"My dear, the tales I could tell." He put the card in his pocket and grinned at me. "Did I see you leave with all three Enforcettes?"

"We were on a mission," I said.

The Captain was called away by a group of fans seeking autographs. Ellin actually smiled at me.

"I've met quite a few potential guests for the morning show,

Randall."

"Great. Where's Camden?"

"I thought he was with you."

We shared a panic moment. In the grip of a particularly strong vision, Camden's been known to wander off into oncoming traffic.

"I'll go this way," I said. She headed in the other direction. I wasn't too concerned yet. Camden had probably gone back to the UFO booth, or he was with the Enforcettes, or he'd been snared by another group of fans who thought he looked like God knows what. You'd think his psychic ability would warn him of danger, but it's useless in that department.

This time, he was okay. As I passed one of the lounge areas, I saw him surrounded by fairies, including the purple Antenna Woman, Diana Davis. He waved me over.

"Randall, come meet the fairy court. They've been telling me about the Dark Feud. Ladies, this is my friend, David Randall."

The fairies greeted me. Although I'd seen her in the hall outside the art room, this was my first good look at Queen Jewel Moonlight. She was even larger than Diana, a woman who looked to be in her forties with waist-length brown hair and brown eyes magnified by thick glasses. Each ear was rimmed with silver hoops, and she had on at least six necklaces, a ring on each finger, and a halo of quivering paper stars.

The fairies made room for me to sit.

"Greetings, elf-friend," the Queen said. "You wish to learn more of this grievous feud between the powers of light and dark?"

Camden gave me a look that said I was going to have to put up with this to get my information.

"If you would be so kind as to enlighten me," I said.

The fairies gave me approving glances. The Queen smiled a benevolent smile. "Then I shall proceed. Twenty years ago, Iris Hudson and I were once friends. She was older than I, thirty to my twenty-six, but we shared a universe of ideas. We loved and respected the works of authors who presented the worlds of faerie. We were going to write our own series of fantasy novels that would revolutionize the entire genre. But, alas, Iris was seduced by the mundane world and its filthy lucre."

All this corresponded to my perusal of the Queen's *Radiant Thoughts.* "That's too bad."

"Yes, indeed. About four years later, after the first *Dark Star* book became famous, she had no more to do with our fantasy world. No more role playing, no more cons—unless she was a paid guest. Our disagreement has passed into fan lore as one of the great feuds. You see, once Iris became famous, she was in a position to help the rest of my loyal subjects in the Seventh Elfin Realm but she never offered any assistance. Many of us, including myself, are excellent writers, but we need a chance. Iris turned her back on all of us. And what is worse, she stole all her best ideas from me and from other contributors to my zines."

"On Saturday, did you stop by her room?" I asked. "Talk over old times?"

She toyed with one of her necklaces. "Mr. Randall, perhaps you're unfamiliar with fan feuds. They are long and unforgiving. She'd made it abundantly clear we were no longer of any consequence to her, so we kept our distance."

"Are any of you staying on the eighth floor?"

They shook their heads. "We're all on seven," Diana Davis said.

"Someone was in the stairwell between the seventh and eighth floors the night she was killed." I turned to Diana. "We have a witness who saw two women arguing about the *Dark Star* books. One was dressed in purple robes."

"Diana?" the Queen said in disbelief. "Were you going to talk to her? After all we'd said?"

Diana looked embarrassed. "I know it's crazy, but I wanted her to sign my book."

"Diana, I am shocked. To speak to that woman after all she's done!"

"I didn't speak to her. She didn't answer our knock."

"Who was the other person with you in the stairwell?" I asked.

One of the fairies timidly raised her hand. "We were just discussing the genealogy of the Wildhaven family in chapter sixteen of book three."

The Queen threw both hands up as if to say, "What has gotten into my loyal subjects?"

"You didn't see a man dressed as the Green Hornet in the stair-well?" I asked Diana and the timid fairy. "Or anyone else?"

They both said no.

The Queen and her fairy court were still reeling from the news of dissention in the ranks. "Diana, I simply cannot believe you would even consider talking to her," the Queen said.

"It's your feud, not mine," Diana said. "Now that Iris Hudson is dead, it's over. You'll have to find someone else to hate." She got up, rearranging the folds of her purple gown, and walked away.

I thanked the fairies for the history lesson. Camden and I followed Diana.

"I'm sorry I got you excommunicated," I said. "Can I buy you a drink?"

Diana debated a moment and then agreed. We went to the food court. I bought everyone a soda, and we sat down at a table.

"Look at me," Diana said. "A forty-five year old woman, dressed like some Thanksgiving Day float."

"There's nothing wrong with a little fantasy life," Camden said.

"I don't know," she said. "There's something so incestuous about fandom. A feud that lasts forever, people still arguing about the same old things, backbiting, jealousy—"

"Just like real life."

She smiled a little. "I've made some very good friends and had a lot of fun, but I think I'm tired of it. When people start getting killed, maybe it's time to get out."

"We still don't know who killed Iris or why," I said. "It may have nothing to do with fandom."

"Of course it does. That's all Iris knew. In case you haven't noticed, Mr. Randall, fandom is one place where looks don't matter. You're appreciated for your brain, your thoughts, your talents, your opinions. If you love a show, and I love the same show, then we're instant friends."

"Or instant enemies, if our opinions clash."

"That's certainly what happened to Iris and the Faerie Queen."

"Is it true Iris stole ideas from her?" I asked.

"Well, that's what she says. I think she's insanely jealous of Iris's success. Iris was under no obligation to help anyone's career, not really."

"So where was the Queen Saturday night?"

"I don't know." Diana looked at me worriedly. "Is she a suspect?"

"I don't know, Diana. How far can you trust a fairy?"

"As far as you can throw her."

After a moment thinking *should we laugh?* we all did.

"Here you are!" Ellin said. "I've been looking for you." She took in the scene of Camden and me drinking with Diana in all her purple finery, and rolled her eyes. "Have you solved the crime? Can we go home now?"

Camden introduced her to Diana. "We just got kicked out of Fairyland, so we needed a drink."

"That makes as much sense as anything," Ellin said.

Diana gazed admiringly at Camden and Ellin. "This is amazing. The two of you together, it's exactly like *Light of Wonder*, when the fairy queen Willow Peace is reunited with Timm of the Light Palace."

"What are you talking about?" Ellin asked.

"Just say 'thank you,' Ellie," Camden said. "It's a compliment."

"Thank you. Time to go, Cam."

Camden said good night to Diana. As he and Ellin walked away, Diana sighed.

"What a lovely couple. I have a picture of Timm and Willow Peace somewhere. I need to read the *Light of Wonder* series again."

"Speaking of stories and pictures," I said. "How well did you know Natalie Montgomery?"

"Not very well. She came to only a few conventions."

"Did her sister Nora ever come with her?"

"I never met her sister. I believe she did the illustrations for Natalie's stories. It's been a while since I've read them." Diana seemed to be lost in thought.

"Something wrong?" I asked.

"I'm still thinking of fandom," she said. "Of how much fun it was when I started with Iris and Jodi and everyone. We met online twenty years ago. My goodness, we were all in our mid-twenties and thirties then. We were good friends once. The oldest fairies are the best." Her eyes began to shine with tears, and she reached in her large pocketbook for a tissue. "Goodness, what's this?" She pulled out a silver pin shaped like an "M." "Oh, I found that in one of the hallways. I meant to take it by the Lost and Found booth."

"I'll be glad to take it for you." I said.

She handed it to me. "Okay, thanks."

As she rooted around in her pocketbook for a tissue, I examined the silver pin. I'd seen a pin exactly like this one on the lapel of Leena Fay's jacket in her artist photo.

"When did you find this, Diana?"

"Oh, sometime Saturday. I don't remember exactly."

I thanked Diana for her help, and she flitted off.

I sat a while longer, thinking it through. Leena had not arrived at the con till Monday, so how was it possible that Diana had found it in the hotel on Saturday?

CHAPTER EIGHTEEN

"When Worlds Collide"

I was ready to go home, but before I left I made my way to the dealers' room and found a man specializing in TV scripts and asked for a copy of "Vats of Orion."

"A real stinker," the man said. "Sure you don't want 'Lost Nebula'? That's a classic."

"Just the 'Vats,' please, and anything else you might have by Terrance Fitzner."

The man looked through another box. "Terrance Fitzner, Fitzner, let's see. Nope. You might try up the aisle at the Crystal Apple."

I paid twelve dollars for a limp copy of the "Vats" script and went up to the Crystal Apple. When I asked about Terrance Fitzner, the man behind the table paused.

"I may have an old paperback by that guy." He rooted through a stack of books sealed in plastic bags until he found a blue book decorated with futuristic houses. "Here you go. *Mission to Starville.* I haven't read it. Sounds pretty corny."

"Do you know anything about the author?"

"No, but he's not anybody famous. This isn't some lost Asimov or anything like that."

Mission to Starville was two dollars. I thanked the man and gave him a couple of ones.

By the time I got home, it was almost five o'clock. Ellin hadn't brought Camden back yet. She'd probably coerced him into another PSN interview. Kary wasn't home, which at the moment was a good thing. I hadn't had time to decide how to explain I'd inadvertently discovered her long-lost half-brother—if that's what O'Conner turned out to be.

I went into my office and sat down behind my desk. How would she react if she suddenly had a new member of her family? He wasn't the best brother I would have picked out for her, but he showed a glimmer of promise. Perhaps Kary could straighten him out. True, the only thing they had in common was a horrible father, but maybe they could bond over that.

Speaking of horrible fathers, it was time to call the pastor and see what he had to say about Darth Vader.

"I've talked with Eric O'Conner," I said when Ingram answered the phone. "He admits he's the Angel of Truth."

"Then I will sue him for everything he's got."

Not exactly what I'd call Christian behavior. "I don't think he's got anything."

"Then what did he expect to get out of this senseless crime? He must want something."

"He's angry because you hate science fiction and fantasy. He compared you to Darth Vader. The villain from *Star Wars*?"

"I know who he is. So that's what he calls me, does he? He associates me with some fictional evil-doer dressed in black with a cow catcher for a mouthpiece? The man is obviously insane."

"He's trying to get your attention. He believes you're his father."

For once, there was silence on the other end of the line. Then the pastor sputtered back. "How dare he suggest that! How dare *you* suggest that!"

"But is it possible? Which is worse? Having your faithful congregation learn that you have a son, or having silly videos on the Internet?"

"This is slander. Trying to blackmail me with no proof."

"He has a letter you wrote to his mother, Gillian Wilson."

Another silence. I could almost hear the steam hissing from

his ears. "Find out how much he wants," he said between clenched teeth.

He ended the call before I could answer. Fine. Let him stew.

After this fun-filled conversation with the reverend, I got out "Vats of Orion." As bad as the episode was on screen, it was even worse on the page. I started *Mission to Starville* and had to put it down. The stilted language, the stereotypical characters, the well-worn setting. It wasn't even worthy of camp status. It was just bad, and interestingly enough, it was just as bad as "Vats of Orion." I checked the copyright date. The book had been written during the height of *Beyond the Asteroids* fame, which was seventeen years ago, three years after Iris left fandom and the Dark Feud began. I guessed that the only way Iris Hudson got this lemon printed was by trading on her fame as a TV writer.

I read "Vats" again, comparing writing styles. Iris had definitely written both. She even used some of the same phrases. "Bow down to your true masters, you worthless worms," was my favorite.

I went to the bookshelf in the island and got Camden's copy of the first *Dark Star* novel, which was written fifteen years ago, a year after *Asteroids* went off the air, and my copy of *Wildflower Wonders,* the fanzine collection of short stories, published by the Fairy Queen twenty years ago when Iris was still a member of the Seventh Elfin Realm.

I opened the *Dark Star* book first. Hudson must have learned a lot from her *Mission to Starville* days, or had a damned good teacher, because this story instantly drew me in. The dialogue was sharp and the descriptions vivid. I turned to 'Unending Starlight,' one of Natalie's stories in *Wildflower Wonders.* As I read, it became more and more evident that Iris had appropriated big chunks of Natalie's work into her own. As for the main female character, Elphinia Day Star, I recalled that was Iris's Seventh Elfin Realm name, and the fact she'd used it in her *Dark Star* series was one of the many things that riled the Faerie Queen.

I usually skip authors' acknowledgments and forwards, but I decided to read the dedication page of *Dark Star.* The author wished to thank a long list of people for believing in her, helping her achieve her dreams, encouraging her and so on. Included in that list was this sentence:

"The author also wishes to thank Natalie Montgomery."

Wishes to thank Natalie Montgomery? Thanking the woman she had plagiarized? Or had Natalie given Iris permission to use her story as the basis for the *Dark Star* novel? If that was true, did Natalie get a cut of the profits? The *Dark Star* series was one of the most successful in science fiction.

As I sat pondering, I heard Kary come in and toss her coat and school bag on the hall tree. She entered my office and flopped down in the chair I have for clients. "That was the longest teachers' meeting ever. How was your day at the convention?"

A nicely loaded question. "Full of surprises," I said.

"Good ones, I hope. Was there a breakthrough in Sean Snyder's murder case? Or Iris Hudson's?"

"It looks like Sean's wife, Natalie Montgomery, is the connection between the two. I think Natalie gave Iris the idea for the *Dark Star* series."

"How did they know each other?"

"They met in Fairyland, writing stories for fanzines. Which reminds me. I need to find out if her sister Nora Montgomery is now going by the name Leena Fay."

"What makes you think she is the same woman?" Kary asked.

"Nora illustrated Natalie's fanzine stories, and the artwork looks exactly like Leena's earlier stuff."

"Is Leena Fay famous?"

"I suppose so. She's famous in the world of science fiction and fantasy art."

Kary indicated my laptop. "Type in 'Famous names of real people,' and see."

"Could it be that easy?"

"Try it," she said. "The Internet is magic."

"Famous names of real people" brought up a wealth of websites with titles like "27 Celebrities Whose Real Names You Never Knew" and "40 Actors Who Don't Use Their Real Names." I had to click through several pages before I found "Authors and Artists Who Use a Pen Name." Way down on the list was Leena Fay aka Nora Montgomery.

"You are brilliant, as always," I told Kary.

She grinned and pushed herself out of her chair. "It's your turn to make dinner. There's some Brunswick stew left in the freezer, or would you rather have a return of the tuna casserole?

"*Return of the Tuna Casserole* sounds like a particularly unappetizing horror movie," I said. "I will thaw out the stew."

***

By the time Ellin and Camden came home, dinner was ready. We took our seats at the table. Ellin was still pleased she'd found more guests for her show and said she might even film a story on the convention itself, complete with the mysterious murder of Iris Hudson.

I hoped the murder wouldn't be a mystery for much longer.

Stuart came puffing in from work. He looked more rumpled than usual, his tie crooked and his nametag askew. "Gosh, what a day! I've been so distracted about this murder thing, I put green peas with green beans and knocked over a whole stack of colas."

"Sit down and take it easy," Kary said. "I'll get you some stew."

"Thanks." He plopped into his seat at the table and wiped his brow. "You haven't caught the killer yet, have you, Randall?"

"Not yet. Sorry."

"That's okay," he said. "I know you guys are doing all you can."

"Are we doing all we can?" Camden asked me in my office after dinner. Ellin was helping Kary wash dishes, and Stuart had gone to bed.

I showed him the silver "M" pin. "Diana found this pin on Saturday. Leena was wearing one exactly like this on her jacket in her artist photo, so I assume it's hers. But it could have been Natalie's." I held it out to him. "Want to see what it says?"

Camden gave the pin a worried look. "If it's been on Leena's jacket, I'd rather not,"

"You don't have to."

"Maybe for a minute." He sat down in the chair and I put the pin in his hand, ready to snatch it back if the visions were violent. He gave a long sigh. "Oh, my God," he said softly, tears welling in his eyes. "The sadness is overwhelming."

"I knew it. Leena is the sad lady Lindsey wants me to help."

"That's all I can see or feel, Randall. If you don't take this back right now, I'm going to start crying and never stop."

I took the pin and passed him the tissue box. "You okay?"

Camden nodded and wiped his eyes. "It was like drowning in tears."

"Pretty sad, then."

"World class."

He blew his nose. "Wish I could tell you more, but I was too busy sinking. I sincerely hope your other clues are not as disconsolate—and you'd better give me twenty-five points for 'disconsolate.'"

"I'll give you thirty-five and another tissue," I said. I handed him the copy of *Mission to Starville*. "Take a look at this and tell me what you think."

He thumbed through the book and read a few pages. "It won't win any awards. Who's Terrance Fitzner?"

"That's Iris Hudson's *nom de plume*."

"Help him, he spoke French. Are you sure?"

"*Oui*. Captain Clark of *Beyond the Asteroids* told me."

"It's terrible, even for an early effort."

"Okay, take a look at this." I slid "Vats of Orion" across my desk.

A few minutes of "Vats," and he grimaced. "Worse than I remembered." He looked on the first page. "Also by Terrance Fitzner. I can't believe the same person wrote the *Dark Star* books."

"I don't think the same person did. I think the real creator of the *Dark Star* books is Natalie Montgomery. Here's Exhibit A." I handed him the *Dark Star* novel open to the acknowledgments page." And here's exhibit B. 'Unending Starlight' by Natalie."

I waited while Camden read parts of both stories. He came to the same conclusion I had. "The *Dark Star* novel and Natalie's story are amazingly similar," he said. "But if Natalie's contribution was this important, why wouldn't she want her name on it?"

"I have a theory on that. Geoff said he and Sean never understood why people preferred fantasy and science fiction instead of dealing with reality. Can you imagine what fun all the psychics and crystal healers and wiccans would have if they knew one of the best selling science fiction series of all time was written by the wife of chief skeptic and debunker Sean Snyder? Also, we knew that Sean was abusive and controlling. The kind of jerk who thought he had a right to control his wife's pursuits, keep her under his thumb."

"So Natalie didn't get any of the credit? What about money? You think Iris paid her?"

"Maybe. Maybe not. If Natalie got a cut of the profits, she would have to explain all those extra dollars to her husband."

"But that's crazy," Camden said. "Natalie must have been terrified of Sean."

"Right. Assuming Leena knew her sister was trapped in an abusive relationship, she might have been real angry about it."

"Angry enough to want revenge on Sean on Friday? And Iris on Saturday? When she wasn't in town until Monday?"

"Are you sure?" I asked. "We don't have any evidence of that. And we do have the pin, found on Saturday."

"That would take planning. You're talking about premeditated murder of two people."

"The Snyders post their schedule on their website, so she could have known they'd be in Parkland for the Con, and at the Psychic Network on Friday for the interview."

"I don't know. I didn't get 'murder' from the pin."

"I need to talk to Vincent Parnell." I said. "As Iris's agent and manager, he took care of the finances. He had to know about whatever deal Iris had with Natalie." I set the pin aside. "In other news, Eric O'Conner has admitted he's the Angel of Truth, apologized to Brianna, and returned the trophy. He also believes Pastor Ingram is his father in a very Darth Vader sort of way."

Camden's reply was a very definite, "No. That would make O'Conner Kary's stepbrother, and I don't see that, at all. I hope you're planning to disprove his claim."

"O'Conner's mother left a note and a letter that may solve this."

"Oh," Camden said. "I hope he wants to bring down the Empire."

CHAPTER NINETEEN

"The Lost Planet"

Wednesday morning, Kary left early for school. I'd spent a restless night, trying to decide what, if anything, to tell her about O'Conner. Camden was as close to her as a real brother, so I knew what he said about O'Conner was true. But I needed more than that to prove Eric was wrong.

I also needed to find out if Leena was in Parkland on Friday night, so that was first on my list. Before I left my office, I checked my desk calendar. Last Friday was the 13th—an unlucky day for Sean Snyder. That made next Friday January 20. Lindsey's birthday.

Once again, the date leaped off the page, this time hitting me with a rush of memories: Lindsey's first birthday, when she laughed and gurgled from her highchair, her face and hands smeared with cake. I'd stuck a bow off one of her presents on her head, and Barbara had fussed, but Lindsey wore it with pride. Lindsey's fourth birthday, when we got her a Disney Princess dress-up box, and she danced around in a gown and tiara for hours.. Lindsey's sixth birthday, a party with all her friends, where she wanted to give all her gifts to her classmate who'd lost everything in a fire.

This is what happens when you keep pushing them back, my reasonable side said. Eventually, the dam has to break. Everything rises to the surface. Enjoy these happy memories. Be glad you have them. If you keep holding them in, you'll explode.

"Could you do that out in the yard?"

For a moment, I thought I'd actually answered myself. But Camden stood in the doorway. "Could get a little messy," he said.

Even though I'm used to him tuning in, it's still unsettling. "I'm not going to explode, at least, not today."

"I didn't mean to pry," he said, "but you were broadcasting pretty loud."

"Yeah, well, January 20."

I didn't need to say anything else. He didn't, either.

I changed the subject. "You told Geoff that Sean was killed by someone he knew. Wouldn't Sean know Natalie's sister? I wonder what sort of relationship he had with Leena, if any."

"Relationship." His expression grew distant. "I almost missed it, but it was there, beneath the overwhelming sadness I got from the pin. There was a spark of anger. Anger toward a relative."

"Her brother-in-law?"

"I don't know. Sadness was the main emotion, but that spark was there, and it was very intense."

"A spark is all it takes."

***

The same young man was at the front desk and looked up with a smile.

"Yes, sir. What can I do for you today?"

"Can you tell me when Leena Fay checked in?" I asked.

He spent a few moments at his computer. "Sorry for the delay. Things have been quite hectic with two murders happening in our hotel. Lots of folks checked out or wanted to move from the eighth floor, which we certainly understand. Ah, here we are. She checked in on Monday."

"Thank you," I said. "What's her room number?"

"Eight-sixty."

"And Vincent Parnell's room number?"

A few clicks of his keyboard and he said, "He's also on eight, sir. Eight thirty-two."

On the eighth floor, I stopped by Leena's room and knocked

on her door. No answer.

When Parnell answered his door, he scowled at me.

"What is it now, Mr. Randall?"

"Do you mind if I come in and ask you a few questions?"

He sighed. "I suppose." He opened the door to let me enter his suite. The bed was off to one side, while the rest of the room included a sitting area with a sofa and two armchairs, a small dining area, and a desk. The desk was filled with stacks of papers. He indicated the stacks. "I'm trying to settle some of Iris's affairs."

"She traveled with all this?"

"A lot of this is notes for her next novel. Go ahead, have a seat, ask your questions."

Parnell sat down at the desk. I took a seat in one of the armchairs. "I'd like to know how you and Iris met."

"I thought I told you. We met while working on *Beyond the Asteroids.*"

"You didn't know each other before then?"

"No."

"Shortly after that, you became her agent and her manager?"

"That's correct."

"This was before or after the *Dark Star* books took off?"

"Before."

That squared with what the Captain of *Beyond the Asteroids* had told me. "Did you continue writing for television?"

"No, I left TV to become her manager."

"Your own books weren't doing well?"

There was a long pause. "Not as well as I'd hoped."

"But the *Dark Star* books were selling like crazy, and as Hudson's agent and manager, you were getting a nice cut of the profits."

"We both did very well, if that's what you're asking."

"What about Natalie Montgomery?"

There was an even longer pause. "What about her?"

"The woman Iris thanks in the first *Dark Star* acknowledgments."

He looked uneasy. "They were good friends."

"I've been catching up on my fanzines at this convention," I said, "and I came across a really interesting story by Natalie Montgomery called 'Unending Starlight.' Something about that story sounded very familiar."

He put both hands out as if ready to push me away. "Now, look. If you're trying to imply there is something illegal here, I will tell you right now Natalie agreed to let Iris use some of her ideas for the *Dark Star* series, and she was adequately compensated for her contributions."

"I think it was more than just ideas for the *Dark Star* series," I said. "I think Natalie wrote the whole damn thing."

Parnell got up and walked to the window where he stood for a while, appearing to decide what to say. When he spoke, his voice was low and tense. "Natalie did not want any credit. She didn't want any money, either. I had to insist that she take something."

"Did Natalie's sister Leena know about this arrangement with Iris?" I asked.

He looked blank. "Her sister?"

"Her name is Nora but she goes by Leena Fay. She's an artist. She illustrated Natalie's fanzine stories. Before *Asteroids*, Iris was in the same fairy fandom group. That's how she met Natalie."

"I didn't know Natalie had a sister," he said, "and I don't know if Natalie told anyone about writing for Iris." He looked uneasy. "I should probably talk to Leena."

"That might be a good idea. She's staying on this floor, room eight-sixty. But she isn't there now. Was Iris okay with Natalie being her ghostwriter?" I asked.

"Not really. But, my God, the money that came rolling in. She certainly didn't want that to stop. Neither did I."

"Natalie died two years ago," I said. "How did Iris keep the series going?"

"Natalie had already completed the next two books," he said. "She also left a draft and notes for another."

"The notes on the desk you said Iris wrote."

He avoided my gaze.

"So there's one more book, and that's the end," I said.

He looked as if he were staring into his own dark star. "Yes," he said. "That's the end."

***

Camden, sitting in the food court, had attracted yet another group of fans who thought he looked exactly like the hero's avatar in the movie version of *Ready Player One*. He was happy to be rescued, and as we made our way to the art auction, I filled him in on my conversation with Parnell and the fact that Leena hadn't checked into the hotel until Monday.

"But did Leena know about Iris's deal with Natalie?" Camden asked.

"Assuming Natalie didn't tell Sean, maybe she didn't tell Leena either."

"And even if she did, why would Leena kill Iris? If what Parnell told you is true, Natalie and Iris were friends, and Natalie was paid for her work."

"But if Leena knew about the deal she might have believed Natalie deserved all the credit and all the money for the *Dark Star* series. We need to find Leena."

We tried the art auction first. Rows of seats had been set up in Ballroom A, nearly all of them filled with excited fans ready to bid on their favorites. Although *Gallery of Fear* wasn't for sale, it was prominently displayed on a stand up front, so Camden and I chose seats as far away from it as possible.

The Faerie Queen and her court were sitting a few rows over. The Queen beckoned. "Good morning, elf friends. Come sit with us."

We joined the fairies in their row.

"Are you bidding on anything special?" the Queen asked.

"No, we're hoping Leena Fay's going to put in an appearance," I said.

"That would be unusual, but you never know. It's certainly a shame she gave up her lovely fairy paintings for such a horrid style."

"Speaking of lovely fairy things," I said, "I found a copy of your zine, *Wildflower Wonders,* and really enjoyed Natalie Montgomery's stories."

The Queen agreed. "One of my very best zines. Natalie was a real sweetheart and a wonderful writer. I'm sure if she'd been given the chance, she would have gone pro."

Natalie had definitely gone pro, but not the way the Queen would have believed. The Queen was back to her favorite subject: herself. "Now, if Iris Hudson had possessed even the tiniest bit of kindness, she would have given me a chance to move up in the publishing world. But I have to admit I enjoy being in control of my writing. I wouldn't want some know it all editor telling me what to change."

Then you probably wouldn't get very far, I thought. "Did you meet with the members of the Seventh Elfin Realm at other conventions?"

"Well, we mainly corresponded by email, but we all used to gather at different cons across the country whenever we could. That was Before."

I could hear the capital "B." The Queen was not going to let go of any past betrayal. "You and Iris, Diana, and Natalie."."

"No," she said. "Natalie never came to conventions. I don't know why."

I knew why. Natalie had met and married the controlling Sean, who was shutting her down.

Another group of fairies came into the ballroom, started toward us, and pointedly changed direction. The Queen sniffed. "Amateurs."

I was beginning to think this woman didn't get along with anyone, either, just like Iris Hudson. "Another feud?"

"At ElfCon Three, they actually stole our idea for the masquerade ball. They're awful. I'll bet you anything they're going to try and outbid me for that unicorn painting. Well, they can't have it. I don't care how much I have to pay."

The auction got underway. The first item was a huge oil painting of the *Beyond the Asteroids* crew in their trademark blue and gold uniforms. As the audience bid and murmured, I found my gaze straying back to *Gallery of Fear*, the harsh colors, the crude canvas with its rough edges.

"I'm going to check for Leena in the art room," I said to Camden. "You stay here and keep an eye on her if she shows up."

I left the Queen forcefully calling out bids for the unicorn painting.

***

Not everyone had decided to attend the auction. Quite a few people were in the art room. The man dressed as a wizard at the desk said he hadn't seen Leena.

"She's probably at the auction," he said.

I wandered through the exhibits and came upon the same young woman who'd first showed me *Gallery of Fear* and answered my questions about Leena a few days ago. She was still dressed Sherwood Forest style and trying to tug a plastic container from under one of the tables.

"Need some help?" I asked.

"I think it's stuck on something," she said.

I lifted the skirt of white cloth and looked underneath. The lid had come up and caught in the edge of the table. "Back it up and I'll close the lid." She did, and I managed to unsnag the container.

She slid it free. "Thanks. I guess I've got too much stuff in it."

There was another large plastic container under the table. "How about this other container?"

"No, that's Leena's," she said.

"Have you seen her today?"

"No, I think she's at the auction."

"When I spoke with you the other day, I didn't realize you were an artist," I said. Some little leafy landscapes were on the table, each framed in pieces of wood. "Is this your work?"

She sat down on the floor beside her box and rooted through the contents. "My Sherwood Forest Series. Do you like it?"

Actually, I did. "Very much. Are those real leaves and flowers in there?"

"Yeah. I like to incorporate natural materials." She gave me a closer look. "Weren't you the fellow asking about *Gallery of Fear*?"

"Yes. Leena is amazing. I was hoping to talk with her again."

"She came in earlier to supervise the moving of *Gallery of Fear* to display at the auction. Of course, there's no way she'd sell her favorite piece, no matter how many people want to buy it." She set a stack of frames on the floor and continued her search through the plastic box.

"What do you have in there? Extra supplies?"

"Yes, you never know when you might need something, or how many prints you might sell. I travel with lots of them." She held up a handful of pictures. "Would you mind setting these up there?"

I put the pictures on the table. Because of the white skirting around the tables, I hadn't noticed the assorted containers underneath. "Do most of the artists travel with boxes like this?"

"Yeah, they're real easy to handle—unless they're too full and get stuck under the table. It saves a lot of time and effort. Otherwise, I'd be carting stuff back and forth from my room all day."

I helped her with more of her pictures and then helped her shove the container back under the table. She thanked me and said she was heading to the auction. After she left, I glanced around. No one was paying me any attention. I went around to the other side of the table where I was partially hidden by a large screen decorated with the same alien fish from *Fatal Fantasy* Buddy had described as "fish critters." I knelt down, and slid Leena's box out. Buried beneath pieces of canvas, brushes, tubes of paint, and other art supplies was a neatly folded gray cloak. Under the cloak was a large knife with a serrated edge.

I had time to take a picture before a crowd of people came down the aisle. I put the cloak back on the knife, arranged the supplies on top, slid the box under the table, and came around the side of the screen in time to appear as if I had been examining the screen.

"Isn't this amazing?" one woman said. "I believe this screen is an exact replica of the one used in *Fatal Fantasy*."

"I believe you're right," I said. "Look at the detail."

"It's quite a find," another woman said.

Quite a find. You could say that.

CHAPTER TWENTY

"The Day the Earth Stood Still"

When I got back to the auction, Camden was standing in the hallway. There was a huge commotion inside the auction room, people yelling and complaining, and other people calling for order.

"Did the elves and fairies go to war?" I asked.

"A brief skirmish," he said. "The Faerie Queen got the unicorn picture, but she was outbid for a Martian landscape. She got into a fracas with the head elf and got punched in the nose. When she saw blood, she fainted. They're trying to settle things now."

"Guess that lets her off the hook. If a nosebleed sends her over, I doubt she could've stabbed Iris Hudson. By the way, ten points for 'fracas.'"

"Thanks. Nothing for 'skirmish'?"

"Okay, ten points for that, too."

We were interrupted by Diana. "Did you boys see the fight?"

"Camden did," I said. "How are things in Fairyland?"

"This will go down in story and song."

"Is the Queen okay?" Camden asked.

"Alive and bellowing. The artist who painted the contested picture said he'd paint another landscape, so the auctioneer was finally able to continue."

"Diana, have you seen Leena anywhere today?" I asked.

"No," Diana said. "Maybe she's in the art room."

"Nope."

"Then maybe she's in her room painting. Oh, there's Captain Clark. I need to get his autograph."

As she hurried off, I told Camden I had news. We moved to a quieter place down the hall from the auction room. "I found a gray cloak in a box under Leena's paintings and a knife, the large serrated variety, useful for cutting canvas and stabbing your enemies. I believe Leena came to Parkland on Friday with plans to kill Sean and Iris. From the Snyders' website, she knew the brothers would be in town for the Con and that they were arriving a day early to appear on the PSN. She also knew they were staying at the Parkland Hilton, site of ExtravaganzaCon. Iris's appearances are listed on the Con program. I'm guessing Leena checked into another hotel and was lurking, in her gray cloak, in the stairwell of the Hilton when Sean came out of his room. She may have asked him for help, gotten him into the stairwell, and stabbed him."

"With the serrated knife you found. But she used Stuart's knife for Iris."

"Right. Here's what I think. During the convention, Leena wore her anonymous cloak with a hood so she could prowl the hallways getting the lay of the land. I don't think she was looking for another knife. But when Stuart ran into Green Hornet around eight pm Saturday night on the eighth floor, she saw the knife in his bag and liked the idea of trying to get the police on the wrong track. She followed Stuart to the hospitality room, and when he left his bag unattended, she took the knife and went back up to Iris's room."

"But as you just pointed out, Iris was supposed to be at the panel from eight to ten, and Leena knew it."

"Yes, but Leena was on the eighth floor, lurking, when Parnell went to Iris's room and got the news that Iris would not deign to attend. Right before Green Hornet knocked into Stuart."

"Ah."

"Somehow Leena got Iris to open the door—maybe by threatening to reveal the real author of her books. It doesn't matter. The point is that Iris surely opened the door." I suddenly realized

I had given Parnell Leena's room number. If he went to talk to her and Leena thought he was part of the scheme to rip off Natalie—"Let's try Leena's room again."

***

As the elevator passed each floor, Camden became more and more anxious. "We need to hurry," he said.

"What's going on? Is she there?"

"Yes, and there's someone with her, but I can't see—there's too much—"

With a "ding," the elevator reached the eighth floor, and as soon as the doors opened, Camden sprinted down and around the halls to room eight sixty. The door had been propped open with the safety latch. I heard scuffling sounds and shouting inside.

"You knew! You knew all this time and never said anything!"

"Let me explain!" said a man's voice. Parnell's voice. Then he cried out, and I heard a thud as if someone had fallen.

Camden caught my arm, but I pushed open the door and stepped inside.

It was as if we'd been transported into one of Leena Fay's ghastly creations. Blood splattered the walls and carpet along with swirls of black paint. Horrible paintings were propped up against the walls and the furniture, graphic depictions of dismemberment, gushing wounds, and monstrous creatures. I realized immediately that what I thought was blood was red paint, but the overall impression was a ghastly display. Camden took the easy way out and fainted right away. The emotional vibes must have hit him like an explosion.

Leena stood over Parnell, staring at him with a strangely fixed expression, a long bloody knife in one hand. Damn! How many knives did this woman have? Parnell struggled to sit up, clutching at a long gash in his arm. Blood streamed down his shirt sleeve.

With a quick move, Leena slashed the knife at him, catching his leg as he rolled away.

I moved fast, putting myself between them. Her eyes looked glassy and not quite in focus. Sweat trickled from her dark hair and down her thin cheeks like tears.

"Do you like my work, Mr. Randall? I call this display *True Angst*. I love the word 'angst.' I've always wanted to use it. I'm sure you can relate to true angst, can't you?"

"I'd feel better if you put the knife down, please," I said as calmly as I could.

She looked at the knife and laughed. "Oh, no. No. I need it to paint with."

I slowly put my hand in my pocket for my phone. "Parnell looks seriously injured. Let me call for help."

"No!" she said and held up her knife. "I'll cut him again."

I pulled my hand back. "What happened?"

She glanced scornfully at Parnell. "He wanted me to know that Iris Hudson truly appreciated Natalie. But that's all a lie. All Iris appreciated was the money, money that should have been my sister's! He's as much to blame for Natalie's death as Iris and Sean."

I wasn't sure how Leena came to that conclusion. "I want to talk to you about Sean."

"He's dead. He deserves to be dead."

"He hit your sister."

She flinched as if I'd struck her. "Not just once. For decades. She couldn't go anywhere or have any friends. She refused to leave him until—until it was too late."

"That's true. But you didn't have to kill him."

"He took her life."

"Natalie died of cancer."

"That doesn't matter. She thought she loved him, and he was a monster. He should have been the one to die, not her. We could have been together again. So I killed him." She began to cry. "It was her birthday."

Dear God.

Leena's words came in an angry rush. "She was so damned weak! I kept telling her to leave him! What took her so long? He kept her from having anything wonderful, and still she loved him." Her voice caught on a sob. A quick swipe of her hand to stop her tears left a smear of blood across her cheek. "And why did she let Iris Hudson take advantage of her? She deserved more than a worthless thank you! I told her to demand that her name be on the cover! The *Dark Star* series was hers, not Iris Hudson's! Hudson stole her ideas, made her do all the work, and took all the credit!"

Parnell groaned, startling us both. Leena took a sideways step. I blocked her way. "He didn't do anything."

"He was just as weak as Natalie! He knew she was the real author. He should have told everyone. He could have stopped it. Why wouldn't he do that?"

The money that kept rolling in, I thought. "Give me the knife and I'll take care of everything," I said. "I'll get Parnell to a doctor, and you can ask him all these questions later."

"Oh, no. Here's what's going to happen," she said. "You killed Parnell, you killed your friend, then you attacked me, so I had to defend myself and kill you."

"Why did I do all that? What story will you tell the cops?"

She hesitated and took a shuddering breath.

"You can't think of a reason, can you?" I continued. "Natalie was the storyteller. She'd know. She'd be able to give me a really good motive."

"That doesn't matter. You'll be dead, too. I'll say you went crazy."

"Nobody will believe you. You have to do better." I reached into my pocket and took out the silver M-shaped pin. "Imagine what your sister would come up with?"

She gasped. "That's Natalie's!"

She leaped toward me and made a grab for the pin, but I kept my distance.

She raised the knife threateningly. "You give me that pin." Her voice was harsh.

"Give me the knife."

"Give me that pin!"

"Hand over the knife."

She shook her head, eyes blazing. "I need it for my next painting."

I moved to put the pin back in my pocket. "Guess I'll keep this, then."

She took a step toward Camden. "I'll kill your friend!"

"Okay, catch."

I tossed the pin to her right. As she jumped for the pin, I clutched her wrist and forced her to drop the knife. She slashed at me with her fingernails. Her thin body was like a steel cable. She hissed furiously, her eyes full of hatred.

"Stop it! How dare you?"

I finally caught her other hand and pulled both hands behind her back. "Your killing days are over."

She jammed the sharp heel of her shoe down on my ankle. I yelped and almost lost my grip. She gave a jerk, and we both slipped and fell. She twisted loose and scrambled for the knife. I jumped over her, but she reached the knife first. She staggered up, panting, readying herself for another attack, then lunged.

I tackled her, grabbed her wrist again, and pounded her hand on the floor until she let go of the knife. I scooped up the knife and backed away toward Parnell, hoping he hadn't bled out.

She crawled across the floor to reach Natalie's pin, then burst into tears. She rolled herself into a ball, clutching the pin.

Parnell was alive, but groggy. I grabbed a towel from the bathroom and wrapped it tightly around his arm, all the while keeping an eye on Leena. Then I called the police.

***

By the time the police arrived and took charge of Leena, Camden was just pulling himself up on his hands and knees. I could only imagine the horrific images bombarding him.

"Oh, my God—Randall—get me out of here."

I hauled him up. "Don't look. Try to think of something else."

"I can't—it's too much."

I got him out in the hallway. There was a sofa by the elevators. "Lie down here. I need to talk to the cops."

He lay down and put his arm over his eyes.

It took a while to sort things out. The EMS team took Parnell out on a stretcher. Two policemen escorted Leena out. She was still sobbing. I explained to Jordan about the cloak and the knife, and how we had found Leena attacking Parnell.

Jordan glanced around the blood-stained room and the row of nightmare paintings. Even his seasoned team looked green, and one young cop had fled the scene.

Jordan frowned at me. "So you're telling me the woman who painted these pictures murdered two people? I believe you."

"She had a lot of pent up anger."

"I'll say. How's Cam?"

"I need to take him home. You know where to find me if you have more questions. Okay?"

Jordan gave us the okay, and I got Camden to the Fury, where he lay down on the back seat. We were about halfway home when I heard him groan.

"I'm going to throw up."

"Not in the car."

"Pull over."

I pulled over and parked. He staggered out to the side of the road and dry heaved for a long time. I helped him back to the car. He lay down with his head in his hands.

"I need Ellie."

I got behind the wheel and started the car. "I'm getting you there as fast as I can." My watch said it was past six. "Is she still at work or at home?"

"At home. Parnell—?"

"He'll be okay," I said. And I sincerely hoped he would be.

CHAPTER TWENTY-ONE

"Riders to the Stars"

Ellin immediately took Camden in her arms and held him, doing her one helpful psychic trick. If he's in the grip of some horrible vision, touching her blanks it all out. Like erasing a blackboard, he once said. After a long while, he sighed, relieved.

"What would I do without you?"

Ellin can be annoyed about this talent. The reason it worked was because she didn't have any extra senses, so nothing was going on in her head that would add to Camden's visions. Today, she was happy to be of service.

"I guess you'd have to hug Randall," she said.

"We may be Galaxy Kings, but we'll take that friendship only so far."

She hugged him again. "Baby, you're still shaking. What did you see?"

"You don't want to know."

Typically, she turned on me. "Randall, do you have to constantly get him involved with these horrible things?" She didn't wait for my answer, but pulled Camden to the couch. "I'll get you a drink."

He kept her hand in his. "Not yet."

She sat down beside him and put her arm around his shoulders. "That bad, huh?"

"The room was filled with such hatred and insanity—it felt like I'd smacked against a wall, a wall full of razor blades."

"That's a cheery image."

"Do you still want to be psychic?" he asked her.

"Not right now."

I snapped my fingers. "Ellin, I have proof you're psychic."

"What?" she said.

"You remember that morning you were making biscuits and you remarked how odd it was that two murders had occurred in the same hotel? Then you said maybe the same person killed Sean. You were right about the murderer. What else could that be but a burst of latent psychic insight?"

She gave me a long look and then laughed. "How about a lucky guess?"

This pleasantly un-Ellin like moment was interrupted by Stuart as he came in from work, looking pleased and relieved.

"Whew! Jordan called to tell me they caught the woman who killed Iris Hudson. I can't tell you how good it is to be a free man! Only now I have to get a new Pik-Ra knife."

"You really want another one?" I asked.

He thought about it. "Well, maybe not. I don't need any reminders of these rough few days, do I? Gosh, I need something to eat."

***

Neither Camden nor I needed something to eat. We let Stuart fix his own supper while the rest of us decided to go to bed. I had just enough energy left to tell Kary everything that had happened before I crashed into a thankfully nightmare-free sleep.

Kary had some sort of half-day workshop the next morning. I didn't hear her slip out. Camden and Ellin were still asleep when I was in the kitchen having a cup of coffee and heard a knock on the door.

I opened the door to find Enforcettes in all their glory. Tiger was wearing a short leopard fur coat. Brianna was in red leather, and Dawn's coat was golden suede.

"We heard all about it!" Brianna said. "Are you guys all right?" I escorted them out to the porch, shutting the front door behind me. "We're fine. Camden and Ellin are having a little quality time right now, but I can fill you in."

"We wanted to thank you for getting rid of O'Conner," Tiger said.

"Even though we wanted to pulverize him," Dawn said cheerfully. "Will we see you and Cam at the con today, David?"

"I think we've had enough con to last for a while," I said.

Tiger gave me a kiss. "I'm sure our futures are entwined. We'll be looking for you at the next one."

They bounced down the steps and got into Tiger's black Firebird. They waved until they were out of sight. They hadn't been gone five minutes when Geoff Snyder arrived, parked behind Stuart's van, and got out. In contrast to his last frantic visit, he walked slowly up the porch steps.

"Randall."

"How are you doing?"

"Better." He reached in his pocket and handed me a check. "I appreciate everything you and Camden did. Who would've dreamed that lunatic sister of Natalie's had so much rage?"

"Come on in."

"No, thank you," he said "It's time for me to go home and get started on *My Last Dance*. I feel I owe it to Sean. He encouraged me to write it. He would want me to write it."

"I wish you every success with it, Geoff."

"Thank you. If I find out someone needs a good investigator, I'll give them your name."

"Thanks," I said. "Sometimes I get lucky."

He fixed me with his fierce stare. "It's more than luck."

"Would you call it supernatural?"

He glared until he realized I was joking. His features relaxed into a reluctant smile. "No, I wouldn't go that far. But you got the job done." He offered me his hand. "I won't forget this, Randall."

We shook hands, and he left. I went back to the kitchen and my coffee. My cell phone rang, and Jordan's name came up. I'd asked him to let me know about Parnell.

"He's going to make it," he said. "You're lucky Leena didn't jump right on you at first."

"How is Leena?"

"Rocking back and forth and singing 'Happy Birthday' over and over, so I reckon she's not all there."

My heart took a little drop and came back up again. "She killed Sean on Natalie's birthday."

"How thoughtful. Is Cam okay?"

"He's with Ellin, so he's fine."

"I need you to come by the station and fill in the rest of the blanks."

"Be there as soon as I can," I said. "I have one more chore to do."

***

Freedom Path United Church of the Revelation still gleamed in the sunlight. The office workers still spoke in muted tones to the faithful callers. I found Pastor Gary in a huge office suite that looked out on the Story Garden. The bookshelves were filled with elegantly bound books and pictures of the pastor shaking hands with politicians and movie stars. On the wall behind his desk was a huge glittering cross made of enough silver to feed every poor person in Parkland.

Ingram was talking with an assistant but dismissed her as soon as he saw me. He shut the doors behind the woman, returned to his desk, and sat down. "Well?"

I put the pastor's threatening letter on the desk. I didn't say anything, just let him read it.

He finished reading and looked up, his face curled in an angry scowl. "So he kept this? That proves he only wants money."

"O'Conner doesn't want any money."

"I don't believe that." He pointed a finger at me. "You tell him if he gets rid of those wretched videos, I won't press charges."

"You're bluffing," I said. "You owe him the truth. If you won't tell it, he has every right to go public. "

His jaw worked as he attempted to control his anger. "Gillian Wilson corrupted my congregation and led one of my most faithful members into sin. I had to save him from this Jezebel. She insisted he was the father of her child, but I convinced him to have nothing to do with her or the child. It would have dishonored the church and ruined his marriage. Any contact would be detrimental."

"So he could have been the father."

"Why would I take the word of a loose woman over that of a good Christian man?"

Not so good if he was having an affair. "Is this man still a member of the church?"

"He left us years ago, an excellent decision on his part."

And possibly helped along by Pastor Gary. "His name?"

"I don't owe O'Conner anything."

"Then he'll always believe it was you."

Ingram fumed silently for a while and then reluctantly said, "The man's name was Howard. Milton Howard. He lives in Atlanta now. That's all I'm going to say."

I had it now. Pastor Gary's reputation always came first. "This would make a great episode for *The Bible Hour*. You could talk about how Jesus was friends with sinners and forgiveness and the love of the church—"

"Don't you preach to me."

"I'm just trying to figure where being a Christian comes in."

"A Christian obeys God's laws!"

"How about the love of money is the root of all evil? I think that's in the Bible somewhere."

Ingram stood, and for a moment, I thought he might leap over the desk and throttle me, but he remained standing, furious. "Get out. Your services are no longer required."

"I'll send you my bill."

On my way out, I decided to have another look in the Story Garden. I wanted to find the angel Kary remembered from her childhood. After wandering the pathways, I found it. There was a woman standing in front of the statue. Her blonde hair was in an elaborate poofed up style, and she had on an expensive-looking pink suit. But something about her made me catch my breath. This had to be Kary's mother. I could see a resemblance, but the woman's face was worn, and her brown eyes looked distant. She heard me approach, came to me, and held out her hand.

"You must be Mr. Randall. I'm Rebecca Ingram. Thank you for helping my husband."

I didn't think I'd ever heard Kary say her mother's name. "You're welcome."

"He told me the man was possessed by demons brought on by the evils of drug abuse."

"That's one interpretation."

"So much evil in the world. One has to be constantly on guard."

"There's a lot of good in the world, too." When she looked skeptical, I said, "Me, for example. I'm the good guy."

"Are you a Christian?"

"No, but I'm friends with one."

She pulled her hand away. "In order to enter the kingdom of heaven, you must accept Jesus as your personal Savior. For whosoever shall call upon the name of the Lord shall be saved, Romans 10:13." She sounded like a robot.

"I'll keep that in mind." She looked so lost, I took a chance. "Mrs. Ingram, I'm in a loving relationship with your daughter, Kary."

She flinched. "I don't have a daughter."

I'm sure your husband has done his best to make you believe that. "She's beautiful and kind and loves trying new things. She's a school teacher and a wonderful pianist."

For a moment, there was a change in her expression. Hope? Regret? Disbelief? It was hard to tell beneath her overwhelming air of sadness.

Sadness.

This was the sad lady Lindsey wanted me to help.

"Kary's also my partner in my detective agency," I said. "She's been a magician's assistant and a superhero among other things. She wants a child, and I'm going to help her find one."

Because that's what I truly wanted.

Rebecca Ingram glanced toward the towering bulk of the church. Then she looked at me. Her voice trembled. "I don't want to go to hell."

"I don't think anyone does."

"For what shall it profit a man, if he shall gain the whole world and lose his own soul? Mark 8:36."

"Would you lose your soul if you spoke to your daughter?"

She didn't answer. She stared at me as if she'd never thought of that.

"Is there something you'd like to say to her?" I asked. "I'll be glad to take the message."

She started to say something, took a shuddering breath, and shook her head. Her face returned to its eerily calm mask. "For the wages of sin is death, Romans 6:23. And they said, believe on the Lord Jesus Christ, and thou shalt be saved, and thy house, Acts 16:31."

I took her hand and gave it a comforting squeeze. "I'll take care of her, I promise."

She didn't say anything else. As I walked away, I took a look back. She stood as still as the angel in the Story Garden, her hands clasped tightly, and tears running down her face.

I don't want to go to hell.

Rebecca Ingram, I thought, I'm afraid you're already there.

***

Speaking of power and thrones, I needed to call Eric O'Conner.

"Ingram's not your father," I told him. "He was protecting a member of his congregation who had an affair with your mother. He says the man's name is Milton Howard. He left the church years ago and lives in Atlanta now."

"Yeah, but he could be lying about all of that."

"That's always a possibility. But if you read the letter again, you'll see it doesn't say anything about Ingram being the accused father. And I have a strong feeling Pastor Gary used his church clout not only to keep Howard from acknowledging you, but also to make the man leave town. I'm pretty good at finding things, so if you'd like me to look into this, I'll see what I can do."

Eric took a long moment before replying. "No," he said. "That is, not now. I'll have to think about it. Is Ingram going to sue me?"

"He said he won't if you take the videos down."

There was a gusty sigh. "When I was little, I thought about my dad all the time, wondering who he was and if he loved me and wanted me. But Ingram—I'm kinda glad he's not my father. And this Howard guy, if he even exists—I don't know, man. Maybe it's time for me to let go."

"Look, those videos were hilarious," I said. "You're really talented. I say, use your powers for Good and move on."

"Yeah, well, all that at the con made me rethink my ideas about vengeance. That was really sick what that woman did, you know? I mean, she took it to the extreme. I don't want to become like that."

"Garnon the Great," I said, "I don't think you'll go that far."

***

At home, Kary's green Ford Fiesta, Turbo, had returned, Ellin's car was still there, and Camden was up and fixing spaghetti. I told him about meeting Kary's mother. "Brainwashed doesn't half describe it."

"I'm sure she's terrified of her husband."

"Just like poor Natalie Snyder." I opened a new pack of paper napkins and put them on the counter. "Camden, you're a Christian, right? How come you're not a screwy robot?"

He stirred the spaghetti sauce. "I think the Ingrams are stuck in the Old Testament, the wrathful, smiting, eye for an eye God."

"So you're New Testament, love thy neighbor and all that. But you don't love Kary's father."

"I'm also a sinner, so that lets me off the hook."

"How convenient."

"Works for me."

I went upstairs and found Kary in her room sorting through a large collection of dresses piled on her bed. "Are you spring cleaning early?"

"Ellin and I are about the same size, so we're trading a few things," she said.

I wasn't sure how to bring up the subject, so I just jumped in.

"I saw your mother today."

Kary put a dress on a hanger and put it in the closet. Her face was almost the same calm mask as Rebecca Ingram's. "How is she?"

She's become a religious zombie. "I told her we had a loving relationship. I think I got through."

Kary hung up another dress. "She always did everything my father said. I used to hate her for not taking up for me. Now, I feel sorry for her—when I think of her. I try not to."

"Maybe someday I can go back in and break her out."

"I don't think you can."

"At least she knows you're safe and has someone who cares for you."

"If that meant anything to her."

I recalled the small sad figure standing in the opulent hallway. The sad lady.

"Oh, it meant something."

"What about my father? Is that business with the videos over?"

"Yes, and he was ever so grateful."

"Perhaps I can show you what real gratitude looks like."

She was leaning in to kiss me when Stuart stopped by the door. "Spaghetti's ready!"

Kary laughed. "Thanks, Stuart." She gave me a quick kiss. "And thanks, David."

"You're welcome," I said. I was always happy to get a kiss from Kary. I was especially happy I didn't have to introduce her to an unexpected and unsettling new stepbrother.

***

At lunch, Stuart entertained us with his police interrogation experience. "I tell you, when I was being questioned that first time, my whole life flashed before me. I mean, I knew I was innocent and Randall was going to prove I was innocent, but still."

"So how was your life?" I asked.

"Really good, actually. No regrets."

No regrets. I thought of Leena Fay and how she must have hated herself for not getting Natalie out of that abusive situation.

Hated Natalie for not being the famous author she should have been, for not being who she wanted her to be. In the end the anger and resentment had driven her to murder. "You're a lucky man, Stuart."

"What about you? Any regrets?" He turned red. "Gosh, that was stupid. I'm sorry. I forgot. Your daughter."

"No, it's okay." I could've let my anger consume me, but I'd managed to work it out without painting pictures of alien flies. "It's better now. Not perfect, but better." I thought of my calendar and January 20. The date no longer glared from the page. It still hurt. It would always hurt. On her birthday, I would always think Lindsey would have been sixteen today, or twenty-five. What kind of teenager would she have been? What kind of young woman?

Now there was another young woman in my life, and I'd promised to find a child for her.

Kary went into the kitchen with Camden to help with the dishes. Stuart leaned forward as if telling a secret. "Cam says his baby might be able to help you. I hope she can."

I had no idea what that meant, only that I wanted to stay and find out. "Me, too, Stuart, thanks."

***

In my dream that night, I could see Lindsey at the edge of the playground. Somehow I seemed closer than before. Lindsey had been skipping rope with another little girl but stopped when she saw me.

Can you help the sad lady, Daddy?

Not Leena. Not Iris. Not Natalie. "You mean Rebecca Ingram, don't you?"

Yes.

I wanted to help Kary's mother. More than that, I wanted to do whatever Lindsey asked.

"I'll find a way," I said. Then I managed to say something else. "Happy Birthday, baby. I wish you could be here."

Daddy, she said with a smile, *I'll always be here.*

End

About the author

Jane Tesh is the author of two mystery series: The Grace Street Mysteries (PI David Randall seeks solace from personal tragedy in a boarding house owned by Camden, a reluctant psychic) and The Madeline Maclin Mysteries (featuring a beauty queen turned PI and her con man husband). Both series are set in North Carolina and are filled with gentle humor and an abundance of colorful rural characters. No surprise, since Tesh's home town of Mt. Airy, NC, is the home of Andy Griffith and is thus the "real" Mayberry. Tesh has also written five fantasy novels published by Silver Leaf books. When she isn't writing, Tesh, a retired media specialist, enjoys playing the piano and conducting the orchestra for productions at the Andy Griffith Playhouse.